"What am I going to do with all this?"

Sam leaned against the kitchen counter and shook his head in amazement at the plastic bins full of sugar cookies, bowls of frosting in pastel colors and every type of sprinkle imaginable.

As much as he wanted to spend the day decorating cookies with Celeste and Parker, he knew it wasn't wise. He had to stop thinking about himself and start thinking about what was best for her. Which wasn't him. She needed a guy who could be there for her in ways he couldn't. He would not be another burden on her.

"Why don't you change, and I'll get everything ready?" Her clear brown eyes held no questions or concerns. Just anticipation.

When he'd changed, he paused a moment in the doorway. Celeste had laid the cookies out on wax paper. Parker was strapped into his portable booster seat. He nibbled on one cookie and banged another against the table. She was spooning the icing into those plastic bags. The Christmas tree twinkled beside them.

What had been an empty cottage had become a warm, inviting home.

What would it hurt if he simply enjoyed being with them today?

Jill Kemerer writes novels with love, humor and faith. Besides spoiling her mini dachshund and keeping up with her busy kids, Jill reads stacks of books, lives for her morning coffee and gushes over fluffy animals. She resides in Ohio with her husband and two children. Jill loves connecting with readers, so please visit her website, jillkemerer.com, or contact her at PO Box 2802, Whitehouse, OH 43571.

Books by Jill Kemerer

Love Inspired

Small-Town Bachelor
Unexpected Family
Her Small-Town Romance
Yuletide Redemption

Yuletide Redemption

Jill Kemerer

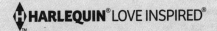

Recycling programs
for this product may
not exist in your area.

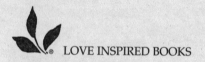

LOVE INSPIRED BOOKS

ISBN-13: 978-0-373-71998-3

Yuletide Redemption

But He said to me, "My grace is sufficient for you, for My power is made perfect in weakness." Therefore I will boast all the more gladly about my weaknesses, so that Christ's power may rest on me.
—*2 Corinthians* 12:9

To my dad, Ron Devereaux.
You always make me smile.

To my mom, Jean Devereaux.
I want to be just like you when I grow up.

To my father-in-law, Leo Kernstock.
You always treat me like your daughter.

To my mother-in-law, Sharon Kernstock.
You bless me in a million ways.

To all those with scars inside or out—
you're loved. Merry Christmas!

Special thanks to Rachel Kent and Shana Asaro
for making this book shine.

Chapter One

Sam Sheffield curled his fingers around the wheel-chair's hand rims and, for the first time in months, tried to fight his bitterness rather than lingering in self-pity. His prayers had gone unanswered, but his family was right. He had to accept his limitations and move forward.

But how?

The bank of windows showcased maize leaves drifting to the deck. Sunshine glinted off the blue waters of Michigan's Lake Endwell. A stunning day in late October. He still loved the lake. At least the accident hadn't taken that. Too much had been stripped away almost a year and a half ago, though. He'd yet to step foot in his auto dealership. Couldn't imagine running the business from a wheelchair.

A knock on the door made him flinch. It must be the woman his sister had mentioned last night. Claire had advised him in her gentle-but-firm tone to be on his best behavior, that Celeste needed a new start. What Claire hadn't said had come through clearly—his family was tired of doing everything for him. It was bad enough Claire had hired a caregiver without his permission, but the bomb his brothers had thrown out yesterday? Turned his blood to ice. He wouldn't think about it. Not now, anyway.

Sam rolled across the hardwood floor. He had no need for a caregiver or personal assistant or whatever his sister wanted to call her. Sure, Claire claimed it was the only way Celeste would stay in the cabin next door for free. But whatever had happened to this girl couldn't compare to what he was going through.

Leaning forward, he winced at the tremors in his leg and opened the door. A willowy brunette stood before him, and Sam moved back for her to enter. With her face shadowed by long dark hair, she took a few tentative steps his way. He held out his hand. "Sam Sheffield."

"Celeste Monroe." Her grasp, like her entry, was elusive, as if she wanted to be as invisible as possible.

He tried to catch a glimpse of her face, but her tucked chin and curtain of hair didn't give him much to work with. Spinning the wheels around, he headed to the oak table. "Have a seat."

She obeyed, not bothering to look his way.

"I saw the moving truck earlier." He splayed his fingers on the smooth wood. "I take it Claire's cabin is working out for you?"

"It's perfect." Celeste pushed her hair behind her ear. Deep brown eyes, nervous, glanced at him.

His breath caught in his throat. *She's beautiful.* "I'm glad you like it."

She smiled, revealing slightly misaligned teeth. Only then did he notice the scars. Jagged silver lines crisscrossed her left cheek and forehead, and one slashed her chin. They in no way detracted from her unusual beauty, and he was tempted to stare, to memorize her face. She bobbed her head, her shiny hair slipping back into position.

A volley of questions flew around in his mind. How had she gotten the scars? Why did she need a new start? What had Claire left out? But the puzzle kept coming back to those eyes—they'd touched a part of him that had been buried since the accident.

He forced his attraction deep down, unreachable. What woman would want a man who couldn't do the most basic life tasks for himself? He couldn't protect her. He could barely take care of himself.

"How do you know Claire?" he asked.

"I don't. Not really. She works at the zoo with my mom's best friend, Nancy, who told your sister about my accident. A few weeks ago Nancy put the word out that I was looking for a cheap apartment. Claire said she had the perfect solution. Basically, I get to stay in her cabin for free if I help you out."

His meddling sister. He wasn't angry, though. Claire couldn't help worrying about him any more than she could control her urge to help Celeste by letting her stay in the cabin.

"You mentioned an accident," he said. "What happened to you?"

"Car accident." The words tumbled out. "My face took the brunt of it. The first five weeks were a blur in the hospital followed by a month in the rehab center. When they released me, I was in no shape to take care of myself. I ended up moving back in with my parents."

"How long were you out of work?"

"I never went back. Until this summer, some issues prevented me from working full-time, and my boss hired someone else anyhow. But I'm working again.

Self-employed. Virtual assistant. I'm hoping to take on more clients now that I'll have my own place."

"The cabin's been empty since June," Sam said gruffly. An accident had ripped her life apart, too. And she didn't look much older than his twenty-seven years. "Claire and her husband moved into a new house. She hasn't had the heart to sell it. I hope she cleaned it for you."

"She did." Celeste cast a sideways peek his way. "You didn't know, did you?"

"Know what?" He itched to return to the windows, to stare past the deck and lawn out to the lake, to let the peaceful view soothe the commotion stirring inside him. Did Celeste mean he didn't know about Claire's arrangement with her? Or something else?

"My face."

The scars. If he wasn't so focused on himself, he would have put it together. It explained the fragile air about her. "Why would that matter?"

"It matters to most people," she said so softly he barely heard her.

Wanting to put her at ease, he lifted his shirt to reveal the right side of his abdomen. He had his own scars, except they'd faded to a dull red. They lashed up and down the length of his torso. "I guess we're even, then."

Her eyes widened, and a breathy "oh" escaped her mouth. "I'm sorry." The way her eyebrows dipped assured him she meant it.

"They're the least of my worries." His physical scars didn't bother him, but the collateral damage from the accident festered. Memories from the conversation yesterday returned with a vengeance. His brothers, Tommy and Bryan, had actually suggested he consider selling his dealership.

Sell his dream?

He balled his hands into fists. Maybe they were right. The accident had been over sixteen months ago, but he couldn't do even simple work tasks. The first time he'd printed out a sales report, his professional goals had seemed so out of reach he'd almost thrown up. He'd printed another one since then, but within minutes he'd broken down in tears. Tears. From him, the man who never cried. But then, he wasn't the man he used to be. He wasn't sure he would ever be more than a broken body.

Celeste's shoulders hunched as she picked at her fingernail. Sunlight spilled into the room, making the table glow.

"I'm glad you recovered enough to work again." He tapped the table lightly. "I don't know how much Claire told you, but I was in a boating accident. The propeller sliced my right side. Severed the sciatic nerve in my upper thigh. The nerve graft wasn't completely successful."

Just speaking those words riled him up. Why hadn't God listened to his prayers? Half of patients like him were able to get around on two feet again. Why couldn't he be one of them?

Well, he *had* been making progress. Before the slip in the shower a few months ago, he'd been walking on crutches, getting closer to graduating to a cane—working hard so he wouldn't need a wheelchair to resume running his dealership.

Let it go. Accept it. Move forward.

"Are you dealing with any long-term issues?" Sam asked. "Beyond the scars, I mean?"

"Some nerve damage. Headaches." Those espresso eyes met his, warming him. "Nothing I can't handle."

He envied her for only having headaches and scars. She had her legs. She could walk.

"When was the accident?" Sam asked.

"It will be a year on December 18." Her attention shifted to her hands.

"The first annual Lake Endwell Christmas parade."

"Excuse me?"

"Sorry." Being trapped in this cottage all the time must have gotten to him. His conversation skills needed work. "The date's stuck in my head. My aunt Sally has mentioned it about fifty times in the last month. December 18. She's on the planning committee."

"A parade." Her chin lifted as she gazed ahead through the windows. He couldn't tell if she liked or hated the idea of a parade. "A nice distraction. I'll be honest—I'm dreading the date."

A twinge of guilt pressed against his chest. Her accident may not have taken her legs, but it obviously had taken a lot from her, too. "I don't blame you."

"How did you get through yours?"

"Through clenched teeth. My family stayed with me all day." Reminding him how much he'd lost. His brothers and sisters went on as usual while his life had been turned upside down. They either spoke in hushed tones, or they faked chipper, everything-is-fine conversations. He ignored their furtive glances and nagging for him to go back to physical therapy. After his fall in June, he'd stopped going, knowing he might never walk unassisted on both legs. The torn ACL and resulting surgery had left his right knee unstable and both legs weak.

A cane, crutches, a wheelchair—all props reminding him he'd suffered permanent damage. He would never carry a bride over the threshold. Even if a woman could see past his disability, what did he have to offer her? Not a whole lot.

"My parents will probably insist on spending the day with me, too." Celeste rubbed her upper arm. "Your family seems nice."

"They are nice. They just don't get the fact I want to be alone."

"I get it."

She was the one person who probably did get it, and for some reason, that made him feel better.

"Yeah, well, my family is tired of me." Sam gave her a tight smile, squaring his shoulders. "You're the only one brave enough to be here right now."

"I'm sure that's not true."

"Oh, it's true. Ask any of them." His family had been taking turns checking on him, cleaning, making meals, doing his laundry and anything else he needed for months. While he appreciated everything they did, he was tired of the strings attached, the incessant hints about physical therapy being at the top of his list.

Maybe they all needed a break from each other.

"Can I get you something to drink?" He wheeled away from the table in the direction of the kitchen, which was part of one wide open area along with the dining and living rooms.

"No, thank you. I'm fine."

He opened the fridge and swiped a bottle of water. Celeste seemed quiet—easy to be around. Not too talkative or demanding. But before he let her into his world, he needed to set some boundaries. After taking a drink, he returned to the table.

"Well, we should discuss the arrangement," he said. "Regardless of what my family thinks, I don't need or want a nurse."

"No one said anything to me about nursing."

"Good. If you wouldn't mind picking up a few groceries for me, doing some light cleaning and helping with my laundry, I think everyone will be happy."

"Oh, no." Celeste faced him, her brown eyes wide. Once more he was struck by her pretty features. "Claire wouldn't be happy at all. When I talked to her a few days ago, she was quite specific."

He squeezed the arms of the wheelchair. "What exactly did she say?"

"Physical therapy at least three times a week. I'm to drive you there and back. And…"

"And what?" He forced himself not to growl. He was going to have a long chat with his sister later.

"I'm not to take no for an answer."

"No."

Celeste expected the negative response, but she didn't expect to sympathize with him. From the minute she stepped into this grand, lakefront cottage—completely wheelchair-accessible, according to Claire—she'd been fighting a losing battle. She'd agreed to be Sam's assistant, because it felt like a God-given gift dropped in her lap. Celeste would get a rent-free home away from the whispers and all the darted looks at her disfigured face. The cabin would make it possible for her to expand her business, take on a few more clients. After all, she had other things to consider now.

She needed to convince Sam to go to physical therapy.

Sam had wheeled his chair in front of the patio door. The wall held floor-to-ceiling windows with magnificent views of mature trees, a rambling lawn and the sapphire water of the lake dancing in the sunlight. An incredible room. And the man with dark blond hair and piercing blue eyes wasn't bad, either. The fact Sam had his own scars to heal made him less intimidating than most of the people she encountered.

Sort of.

But whether he was gorgeous or not wasn't the issue. If she wanted to live in Claire's cabin, she had to follow Claire's rules. "What's wrong with physical therapy?"

"It didn't work." His profile could have been etched in marble.

She thought back to what Claire told her, and something wasn't adding up. "What do you mean?"

"All my progress was for nothing."

"But you were making progress?"

"I'll always need a wheelchair." His lips drew into a thin line.

Should she continue this obviously touchy subject? If she didn't, he might refuse physical therapy. Claire's cabin meant a life of her own. Privacy. A reprieve from what her life had become. She couldn't depend on her parents forever.

The plastic surgeon would reevaluate her at the follow-up appointment on December 16. Then she'd have another operation to reduce her scars. Who cared that he had already warned her he didn't recommend further surgery? The appointment would prove him wrong. It had to.

This handsome, hurting man in front of her—the one who'd been given a crummy deal the same way she'd been—only made Celeste want her old face back more. She'd never been a supermodel, but men used to notice her and little kids didn't ask awkward questions. She couldn't imagine a romantic relationship in her current skin. It had been hard enough in her old one. More surgery was vital. Living here, away from unwanted attention, was, too.

She squared her shoulders. "You're not paralyzed, correct?"

"No. Not paralyzed." He flexed his hands. "I slipped in the shower back in June. Tore ligaments in my right knee. Had to have surgery on it."

Her heart tightened at all he'd been through. *Lord, I'm sorry for all the ways I pity myself. Please help Sam.*

"Claire mentioned the possibility of using a cane." It had been a while since she engaged in conversation this long with a stranger. She clasped her hands in her lap.

"My doctor didn't make any promises."

"Doctors can't really make promises," she said quietly. Hers certainly hadn't. "What did yours say?"

"With enough physical therapy, I *might* be able to get around with a cane eventually. I'll need a wheelchair or crutches to give my leg a break when the pain gets bad."

"I'm sorry. I take it you can't walk at all?"

"For short periods. With crutches."

"That's good." She nodded.

"I haven't used them much since I fell."

"Oh. Does the doctor want you off your leg so it can heal?"

He didn't meet her eyes, but his right shoulder lifted in a shrug. "It's less painful this way."

Not exactly the answer to her question. "But how will you get better if you stay in the wheelchair?"

"There's no getting better. I won't be able to do the things I used to do. I'll never run, ski or slam-dunk a basketball again."

Heat climbed her neck. It wasn't her business. She was here to help him in exchange for the cabin. Nothing more. But she really couldn't follow his way of thinking. He refused to go to physical therapy, but without it he'd always be in a wheelchair. *Hmm...*

"I don't know much about it," she murmured.

"I don't want to be confined to this chair, but I can't risk permanent damage."

"So let me take you to physical therapy."

"No."

"But you just said—"

"I'd give anything to walk again. Hobbling around with a cane isn't walking. It's a rotten consolation prize."

"I'm really confused. You have a chance to improve your life." She let the rest of her thought go unspoken. *But you're too proud to see a cane as an improvement.*

He jerked his head to the side. "I don't want this life."

And there it was.

Now Celeste understood why Claire had offered an empty cabin in exchange for help with Sam. Until this moment Celeste had worried the offer was only made out of pity. But if pity played a part, Claire's concern for her brother was clearly the bigger factor. This man had been through so much, and he hadn't reconciled his past to move on to the future.

"What do you want?"

He didn't answer right away, but he sighed. "I was the CEO of Sheffield Auto, our family business. Making decisions for five auto dealerships, including one of my own. Everything was going great. Then one day I go fishing with my friend, and nothing has been the same since."

Celeste nodded in sympathy. He'd had big goals. Unlike her. Until last December, she'd been drifting along, working for an insurance agency and living in a dinky apartment. Her degree in history had been filed away in a box, unused. Lately she'd been thinking of dusting it off to become a teacher. Be the woman she could have been.

But not with these scars. She'd be the laughingstock of the school.

"My life isn't the same, either. I don't think it ever will be." She focused on a chickadee perched on the deck railing outside. Another joined it and they flew off together. Escaping. Lake Endwell was her escape.

"I haven't figured out how to move forward." With his elbow propped on the table, his chin rested on his fist.

"Do you still want to run your dealership? And be CEO?"

"Not from a wheelchair."

Her gut told her this man needed physical therapy as badly as she needed more surgery on her face. But how could she convince him?

"What about returning to work with a cane? You have options." She tipped her head. "Try physical therapy again. Claire won't let me live in her cabin unless you do."

"My sister?" He scoffed. "She wouldn't kick you out."

"She would. She's determined to get you back to PT."

"I'll find you another place to stay."

"I don't want another place." She didn't know why this man was touching such a nerve in her. She could live somewhere else. But the dark circles under his eyes shot compassion through her heart. She wanted him to smile. Wanted him to have hope. And her approach clearly wasn't working. "Look, I need this."

"Why?"

What was the saying about desperate times and desperate measures?

"I'll show you." She prayed this didn't backfire as she walked out the door.

* * *

Sam rubbed his forehead as the door clicked behind Celeste. For a soft-spoken person, she sure knew how to say things that barbed right to his soul. He wasn't angry. Wasn't even upset. For months he'd carried a Dumpster full of excuses on why he should give up. Why physical therapy wasn't for him.

And for what? He kicked the table leg with his good foot. This was no way to live.

If he didn't return to work after Christmas, there would be no work to return to. His brothers had told him they couldn't continue to help run his dealership. They each had two of their own, and they'd given up most of their free time to keep his profitable.

He would be forced to sell the dealership. They would name a new person to step in as CEO. Succeeding in this business took a hands-on approach and a special personality—one Sam used to have.

Maybe that was the real problem. He'd lost his courage. Lost his identity. Maybe it *was* time to try physical therapy again. His bones ached thinking about it. Getting around in the wheelchair wasn't ideal, but it kept him from the relentless aching and stiffness PT brought on.

Besides, his weak knee could very well cause him to fall, putting him at risk of tearing open the healing sciatic nerve. He'd fought hard to regain feeling in his foot and lower leg. Portions of it were still numb. He might not be moving forward, but at least he wasn't in danger of a permanent setback—paralysis.

The door opened with a creak. Sam sat up straighter, not believing what he was seeing.

Celeste held a dark-haired child in her arms. The baby rubbed his eyes and let his head fall back against her shoulder. He wore little navy pants and a lime-green shirt. A diaper stuck out from the top of the elastic, and his feet were strapped into tiny running shoes.

Sam's heartbeat paused at the picture they presented. She had a baby.

Longing for a child of his own slammed in his gut. He closed his eyes briefly, willing the futile emotion away.

No wonder she needed a new start. It all made sense now.

Celeste padded forward. "Is it okay if I sit on the couch?"

"Of course." He followed her to the leather couch and chairs. A sweet smile graced her face as she stroked the sleeping child's hair from his forehead.

"This is my nephew, Parker. His mom was killed in the accident."

Sam's mouth dropped open. Wasn't expecting those words. A nephew. The accident. Had Celeste's sister been killed?

"Brandy and I were best friends ever since we sat next to each other in first grade. My big brother, Josh, started dating her after we graduated from high school. They got married four years ago—Josh was deployed off and on throughout their marriage—and then they found out about this little bundle of joy."

"I don't know what to say. I'm sorry." His mind reeled. Here he'd been having a pity party about his leg, not realizing Celeste had lost her best friend. Her sister-in-law.

"I am, too. It breaks my heart every day knowing Brandy and Josh are missing Parker's life."

"Josh? Was he in the car as well?"

She shook her head. "No. He was killed overseas a few weeks after finding out Brandy was pregnant. Roadside bomb in Afghanistan. After he died, Brandy got really depressed. She was obsessed with making up a will. Of course I agreed to be Parker's guardian, although I thought she was a little too intense about it. But here I am. Raising Parker. Permanently."

He could barely take it in. "So your brother never got to see his baby?"

Celeste kissed Parker's head. He slept soundly on her lap, his cheek still resting on her shoulder. "No, and it breaks my heart. I wish he could have. He would have loved his baby. I miss him."

"Don't you have family who could raise him?" He couldn't imagine taking on such a big responsibility so soon after an accident.

"*I* want to raise him. I promised Brandy. My brother and I were close, and I consider it an honor. Besides, my parents both work full-time. They're getting older, and they don't have the energy I have."

Sam hesitated. "Why is it so important for you to live in Claire's cabin? Why here?"

Her pretty brown eyes dimmed. "I need to create a life of my own." She wrapped her arms tightly around Parker. "I guess I need some time away from it all. Losing my brother and my best friend. Getting used to this face. It's hard when people see the new me but mourn the old me with their eyes."

He understood what she was saying. It was why he hadn't left the cottage in a long time. People expected to see the Sam with a quick joke who could stand tall and play volleyball at a picnic. Seeing him in a wheelchair made them uncomfortable. Or maybe it made him uncomfortable. Maybe both.

"Yes, that's a good way to put it," Sam said. "I guess neither of us got what we wanted out of life."

"I guess not." She tugged Parker's shirt down over his back. "But I'm going to be the best parent Parker could have in this situation. I'm going to make sure he knows everything about his mommy and daddy. Brandy would have done the same for me. And Josh—well, I'd do anything for him."

Sam thought of his four siblings. He'd do anything for them, too.

He'd been selfish. It was time to start thinking about someone other than himself. He had an opportunity to help Celeste. And the baby in her arms.

"Okay, I'll go to physical therapy."

"Really?" Celeste blinked, then beamed.

Man, she was pretty. "Yeah."

"Good. I hope you don't mind Parker riding with us. I'm kind of all he has."

"I like kids." The desire for one of his own hit him again. "How old is he, anyway?"

"Just turned a year. He's almost walking. Claire told me there are plenty of babysitters she can recommend if you don't want him underfoot when I'm cleaning or helping you."

"Save your money. He's welcome anytime. It will be easier for all of us. Why don't you give me your phone number, get settled next door and come back in a few days. We'll work out a schedule then."

Celeste stood, jostling Parker, and rattled off her cell phone number. He typed it into his phone. She carried the baby to the door. "Sam?"

"What?" He followed her, waiting as she stood in the open doorway.

"Thank you."

"For what?"

A blush rose up to her cheeks. "For understanding."

Once she left, he stared at the closed door for a long time. If she had the courage to raise a little boy and continue with her life after being in a terrible accident and losing her best friend, maybe he could find it in himself to try again.

Because he didn't want to spend the rest of his days in a wheelchair.

Chapter Two

"Well, that was unexpected." Celeste breezed past her mother through the hall to lower Parker, still sleeping, into the portable crib she'd set up in the second bedroom. Their new home. Her first step of independence in a long time. How she wished she could call Brandy and tell her every last detail about Sam and the cabin and… She choked down the lump forming in her throat. Brandy was gone, and Celeste was to blame. Living without her best friend didn't get easier. She suspected it never would.

For now, though, she needed to get the house in order. Start fresh. Put the past year behind her.

After kissing her fingers and pressing them against Parker's forehead, she returned to the living room, dodging a pair of burly guys who carried boxes to the kitchen.

"It didn't go well?" Her mom cleaned the inside of a cupboard with a disinfectant wipe.

In black yoga pants and a hot-pink sweatshirt, Shelly Monroe looked younger than fifty-five, but then, she'd always been a believer in drugstore hair color, mascara and fuchsia lipstick.

"Was he unfriendly or something?" Mom sat on the recliner, which was swathed in clear plastic, as Celeste collapsed on the matching couch.

"No. He was…" Celeste didn't know how to describe him. Wasn't sure what her impression was yet. The only thing she knew for certain? She anticipated seeing him again. "Well, for one, he's really good-looking."

"Ooh." Mom's face lit up. She pretended to lick her index finger and made an imaginary mark in the air. "A point in his favor. Bonus. What else?"

"He's in a wheelchair, but he's not paralyzed." Celeste twisted her hair back and secured it with an elastic band. "But it sounds as though physical therapy won't cure him, at least not entirely. I think he's been depressed. You know how it is."

"I do." Mom's brown eyes filled with sympathy. "You'll be good for him."

"We'll see." She shrugged. "I got him to agree to physical therapy, so I don't have to worry about losing this place."

"His family will be relieved. And it will get you out more, which makes me relieved."

Celeste didn't respond. How could she admit she only planned on driving him to and from the rehab center? She wasn't stepping foot in the place—or any place, for that matter. All the shopping Sam needed she'd do as early as possible to avoid people staring at her.

"I know that look." Mom drew her eyebrows together, pursing her lips. "I'm still not thrilled about you moving here, but since you have, I hope you'll try harder to get out and about. Your scars have faded so much. You don't need to be self-conscious."

She wanted to yell, *"You go out there with slashes across your face and tell me I don't need to be self-*

conscious. You don't know!" but she held her tongue. She loved her parents. She'd probably say the same thing if she were in their shoes. "I'll try."

Mom reached over and patted her knee. "I know it's hard on you. I hope you'll go to the church Claire mentioned. It might help."

"I have my Bible, Mom. I pray. I'm closer to Him than ever."

"I know. It's just…well, studying on your own isn't the same as having fellowship with other believers."

Not this again. "One thing at a time, okay?" Celeste missed going to church. Another reason she desperately wanted more plastic surgery. Maybe next year would bring the new life she craved. The one where she could go out in public without feeling like an exotic creature at the zoo.

Sam's pinched face came to mind when she'd asked him about his injury. She couldn't really blame him for being upset at the way his life had turned out. If he'd never be able to walk on his own and do all the things he must have loved, why would he be excited to go through the hard work of physical therapy?

Both of their lives were on hold. And they had taken a far different turn from what either of them had expected. She got it. She did. She felt a special bond with him because of it. Had he felt it, too?

"Does Sam have a girlfriend?"

"I don't know." And she wasn't going to find out. Between her disfigurement and her nephew, she couldn't imagine dating anyone. Especially not the cute guy next door. She lacked flirting skills, anyhow. The feminine gifts women seemed to be born with had escaped her. Too often, she was tongue-tied and awkward on a date. No, she didn't see a boyfriend in her future. But, hypothetically, if she did picture one, he looked exactly like Sam Sheffield. "I'm here to help him out. Nothing more."

"You never know," Mom said in a lilting voice. The set of her chin meant she was ready to dig into the topic.

"I do know." Celeste stood and began peeling the plastic off the couch. "Dating, romance—I can't deal with any of that right now. I have enough on my plate as it is."

"When the right guy comes along, you'll be ready." Mom helped her yank the plastic off. "Maybe he's next door."

She fought the urge to roll her eyes, even if the idea made her heart beat faster. "I'm his personal assistant, driver, shopper—whatever he needs. That's it. In the meantime, I need to get at least two more clients for my virtual assistant business."

Her mother made a face, so Celeste jumped in before she could speak. "And I've decided to look into teaching history."

"Really?" Her mom's eyes widened, looking suspiciously moist. "That's wonderful!"

"But first I'm waiting to see what Dr. Smith says."

Mom clamped her mouth shut, arching her eyebrows. "He's already told you. You need to let it go."

She pivoted and marched to the kitchen, shoving the wad of plastic in the trash before returning. "And everything I've read said to wait twelve months, get reevaluated and make decisions then. My condition might change."

"What if it doesn't?"

"It will."

"Celeste—"

"Let's drop it."

"I don't want you getting your hopes up only to be devastated." She stepped forward and cupped Celeste's chin with both hands. "You're beautiful."

Celeste jerked away. Beautiful? Only a mother could say that.

She had a mirror. She was not beautiful.

Mom continued. "Josh's benefits should be enough to cover your basic expenses, especially since you don't have to pay rent. Dad and I have your medical bills almost paid off, so don't worry about money."

Celeste hugged her mom. "Thank you."

"You don't have to thank us. We're blessed your insurance covered as much as it did."

"But still… I want to pay you back."

Mom shook her head and patted Celeste's cheek. "Dad and I can afford it. We both have good jobs. You worry about yourself and the baby."

When she had enough clients to support herself, she planned on setting aside money for Parker's college fund. In the meantime, she'd research what it would take to get certified as a teacher.

Mom pushed up her sleeves. "It might take Parker some time to get used to this change, too."

"Yeah, I know." She was new at this parenting thing. She'd been caring for Parker while living with her parents, but they'd helped her when they got home from work. Would she be able to do this all by herself?

"We're only half an hour away. Call if you need anything. Dad and I will come by a few nights a week, and we'll take him anytime you need a break."

The sliding door leading to the deck opened, and her father, Bill Monroe, stepped inside. "Is your mother giving you a hard time?" He kissed the top of Celeste's head and squeezed her arm. "You doing okay, kiddo?"

The tension in her neck dissolved. Dad had always been her champion, the one she ran to when life got her down. Since Josh's death and the accident, worry lines had dug deep around his eyes, but his tall, trim figure and thick gray hair still gave him a vital appearance.

"I'm fine, Dad. Just got back from Sam's. He's the first person I've met in a long time who has as many, if not more, problems than me."

"I'm sorry to hear he's struggling. Sounds like he needs your help."

"Thanks, Dad." She wiggled one arm around his waist and leaned her head against him.

"Nice yard you've got back there. You'll have to watch Parker with the ornamental pond, though. It's wider and deeper than it looks. It only takes a few inches for a child to drown."

"Do you think we could fence it off?"

"We have to do something. I'll run over to the hardware store." He patted his back pocket to check for his wallet, then pulled out his keys. "Be back in a few."

Mom returned to the kitchen and unpacked glasses. "Are you sure you can handle Parker? If it's too much for you, say the word and we'll move you home with us."

She grimaced, shaking her head. "I need this, Mom."

"But—" Concern glinted in Mom's eyes.

"Don't worry. If my headaches get bad again, I'll consider it, but I don't think it will be an issue. They've been much better since summer."

"Okay, okay." Mom stretched on her tiptoes to place a glass on the upper shelf.

Celeste stripped packing tape off a box in the kitchen and stacked plates in a cupboard. This cabin felt like home already. And knowing she wouldn't run into any-one from her past took a layer of pressure off. All the rumors about the accident had gotten back to her over the previous months. Variations on the same theme—she'd been either texting or negligent or intoxicated before the car jumped the ditch and wrapped around a telephone pole.

A shiver rippled over her skin. No, she hadn't been texting or drinking. But if she'd paid more attention to the weather conditions, she would have realized the pavement was covered in black ice. She would have driven slower.

And Brandy would be alive.

The plate in her hand slipped. She tightened her grip.

When she got the surgery and no one could see the scars anymore, they would forget about the accident. She'd be able to face herself in the mirror. She could look at Parker and not want to crush him to her, crying out, "It was my fault! I killed your mommy!"

She'd lived with the visual reminders for too long. They'd forced her into hiding, away from the options that used to be available to her. Her mind flipped to Sam, his comment about not wanting his life.

She didn't want hers, either.

The life she wanted depended on more surgery.

Sam wiped the sweat off his forehead with a towel Saturday morning. The clock read 9:20, which meant he needed to get ready. Celeste would be here in ten minutes to work out a schedule. *Schedule.* The word brought a bad taste to his mouth. It was impersonal, reminding him he was a duty, nothing more. It had been three days since Celeste moved in, and he hadn't been able to get her or Parker off his mind.

He tightened his hold on the crutches as he clip-clopped to the kitchen. Regardless of what his family thought, he hadn't completely given up on himself. Every morning he spent an hour performing range-of-motion exercises and working his upper body with weights. The effort always exhausted him, and the pain in his legs? Excruciating. He dreaded returning to physical therapy next week.

Maybe he should cancel.

And break his promise to Celeste? If he was that much of a coward, he might as well give up on life now.

He'd go to PT. He was a fighter.

Was being the key word.

When was the last time he'd fought for anything other than to maneuver his body out of bed without aggravating his leg? Lately he'd played the role of invalid a little too well.

Fumbling with the cupboard door, he almost dropped his crutch. It had been a long time since he used them to get around the cottage. Both arms and legs already ached. Whenever he put weight on his bad leg, his ankle rolled and knee caved. Balancing on his left leg and crutch, he pulled a glass out of the cupboard and flipped on the faucet, letting the water stream until it ran cold.

In some ways he'd been fortunate. Within six months of his first surgery, he'd regained feeling in his foot. Most of his leg followed. He'd used crutches until June, when one slip in the shower had thrown him back to square one. The ligaments in his right knee had torn and the healing nerve graft had been strained. Another surgery had repaired the knee, but three weeks with his leg immobilized had set his progress back considerably. The physical therapist made home visits for two weeks, but when the home visits stopped, so did Sam's motivation. The flexibility and strength he'd fought so hard for had declined.

What if physical therapy didn't work? Why do it if he'd be stuck in this state forever?

You promised her, Sheffield.

Now and then he'd caught glimpses of Celeste carrying Parker across the lawn to the edge of the lake. Her hair was usually pulled back, and her face would glow as she held both Parker's hands so he could toddle in front of her. He wished he could join her and toss Parker up in the air and catch him the way Tommy did with his youngest, Emily, who would giggle nonstop.

Sam frowned, thinking of Parker's dad. The kid didn't have a father, and Celeste appeared to be single. He hadn't seen any cars besides her parents' pull up.

He changed into a clean T-shirt and checked his appearance in the bathroom mirror. Too thin and pale with dark smudges under his eyes. In other words, a train wreck. The sensation of pins and needles spread across his right knee as a faint knock came from the kitchen.

Crutches or wheelchair? Experience said to settle his leg on the footrest of the wheelchair or he'd be in for a world of hurt, but vanity won. He thunked his way down the hall and hollered, "Come in."

Celeste stepped inside with Parker on her hip and her head lowered. When she glanced up, Sam's lungs froze. Maybe it was the shyness in her brown eyes or the slight imperfection in her smile—whatever it was, she affected him. If his life was different, he'd be tempted to ask her on a date.

The muscles in his stomach tightened. His life wasn't different. He couldn't even handle leaving the cottage. How could he fantasize about dating?

"You're up and about." Celeste sounded surprised. The day was sunny but cool, and she wore a beige cardigan over dark jeans and matching beige slip-on canvas shoes. "You look pale."

Yeah, a mere hour of exercises left me limp.

"Come in and sit down." He led the way to the living room and sat on a chair. He made a conscious effort not to hiss as he lifted his bad leg onto the ottoman. *Sweet relief.* The aching lessened but the tingling sensation increased.

She perched on the edge of the couch and bounced Parker on her knees. Sam peered more closely at him. His eyes were lighter brown than hers, and he had chubby cheeks and a happy air about him. Sam had the craziest urge to take the boy in his arms and set him on his lap.

"Cute kid." He smiled at him, then studied Celeste from her shiny hair to her slim frame.

"Thanks." She seemed to be aware of his scrutiny and shrank into herself. She nodded to his leg. "How are you? Are you feeling okay?"

"I'm fine."

"Are you sure? You're not in pain?"

Here he'd been trying to appear somewhat normal, and he'd obviously failed. She viewed him as a patient. Not as a man.

"Did you bring your calendar?" he said. "Let's figure out a schedule."

"I keep everything in here." She held up her phone.

Phone. His was in the bedroom. As much as he wanted to get it himself, the sensations in his leg screamed not to. "Mine is in my room. Would you mind getting it for me?"

"Sure." She rose, taking Parker with her. The boy watched him over her shoulder. Sam almost waved at the little guy.

"First door to your right. It's on the table." Next to his hospital bed. A further reminder he was an invalid. Real men didn't sleep in beds with railings.

Why was his pride flaring up now? She'd see the entire house when she cleaned. Would he feel the same if Celeste were older, unattractive, unavailable? Probably not.

If he could go back in time, back to when he was whole...

"Here you go." She handed him the phone, her slender fingers brushing his.

"Thank you." Ignoring the way his adrenaline kicked in at her simple touch, he swiped the screen and clicked through to his calendar. "Why don't we start with cleaning?"

For the next ten minutes, they hashed out a schedule. Toward the end, he struggled to concentrate. His leg had been growing stiff as they talked.

"Could you grab me an ice pack from the freezer?" He grimaced, shifting to ease his discomfort. "It slips into a wrap." Beads of sweat broke out on his forehead. When would this get easier?

She set Parker on the area rug a few feet in front of him, went to the kitchen and returned, handing Sam the ice pack. "Is there anything I can do? You look like you're hurting."

He was. Every day brought pain. "The ice wrap will help. I overdid my exercises this morning."

She helped him fasten the wrap on, and he leaned back in the chair, closing his eyes and counting to five. If she said anything, he didn't hear it. When the worst of the pain passed, he opened his eyes.

Parker still sat on the rug, but his little legs pumped back and forth as he laughed, both fists full of the fluffy material. Sam's discomfort faded at the sight of such delight.

"You do exercises?" She resumed her spot on the couch, leaving Parker where he was to enjoy the rug.

"I did physical therapy nearly every day for the first year after the accident. I was making decent progress until I fell almost at the year mark. Ever since the operation in June, my knee's been weak and stiff. I still do a sequence of exercises each morning." It wasn't enough. He knew it. Had known it for months. But the longer he stayed away from therapy, the more daunting it became.

"I had to learn how to eat again. A few spots are painful to touch." She pointed to the scar on her cheekbone then to her chin. "It's hard." Her tone softened. "What you're doing is hard."

It was hard. No one understood how hard.

Except maybe her. Which made him like her even more.

"Can you drive me to the rehab center next week?" he asked gruffly. "I have appointments scheduled Monday, Wednesday and Friday. Ten o'clock each morning."

"Sure." She typed the information into her phone. "Anything else?"

"Not right now." He wasn't ready for her to go, though. She distracted him from the monotony his life had become. "Tell me about your life before the accident."

"There's not much to tell." Celeste rummaged through the diaper bag and handed Parker a small stuffed dog. He promptly shoved the ear in his mouth. "I answered phones for an insurance agency. My major didn't exactly help my job prospects."

"What was your major?"

"History."

"You don't want to teach?" His muscles loosened as the ice worked.

"Actually, I've been thinking about getting certified." She gave him a shy glance. "It depends. A lot has changed."

Parker squealed and the floppy dog flew through the air. He crawled after it. Sam grinned. Yes, he could see how things had changed. She had a baby to care for.

"What about you?" she asked. "Do you think you'll work again?"

The thought of not working again horrified him almost as much as the thought of living out his days in a wheelchair. "Yes."

"The dealership?"

"Uh-huh." He tightened the wrap. As much as he'd tried to deny it, he craved his job. He'd been toying with the idea of printing off last month's profit-and-loss statement again. Maybe this time he could get through it without vomiting. "I oversaw Sheffield Auto. My brothers and I had meetings every Friday morning at the closest dealership—one of Tommy's—to go over quotas, employees, budgets, you name it."

And he'd been in charge. Finally a respected part of the family business instead of the pesky little brother. Man, he missed it.

"Do you miss it?"

It was as if she'd read his mind.

"Yeah."

"You should go to one of the meetings."

"I don't know." He frowned as the view of his propped leg greeted him. He'd gone from annoying little brother to respected member of the company to cripple. He was afraid of breaking down in front of his brothers and dad. Could he return to the job he'd thrived on?

Parker hauled himself up to a standing position, then fell back on his bottom. He chewed on the toy again.

"Would they come here?" she asked.

They probably would. But he wanted out of this cottage. Wanted to be the CEO, not the victim.

Was he capable, though? The accident had injured him in ways he didn't want anyone to know. "I'll see how I'm feeling after a couple of weeks."

Her sweet smile made him want to declare he would be at those meetings, but he knew better than to make promises he couldn't keep. The only thing worse than being pitied would be for Bryan, Tommy and Dad to witness him having an emotional breakdown.

The last thing he wanted was another devastating setback. He had to be careful, which meant playing it safe and taking things slow with his leg—and with his life.

Monday morning Celeste craned her neck to peer over the counter. Parker sat on his play mat and grunted as he gripped a toy airplane over his head. When he shook it, music played and lights flashed. She had five minutes before she had to buckle him into his car seat. Today was Sam's first day of physical therapy, and she'd promised she'd get him there early. A thrill of excitement sped through her veins at the thought of seeing him again. He had a kind heart. It matched his face, which kept flashing before her when she closed her eyes at night.

He was way out of her league. Too handsome, too next-door, too everything.

She frowned at the drizzle outside. Sam had already told her he would be in the wheelchair since he couldn't take the chance of hurting his leg using the crutches.

What if he slipped getting into her minivan? And would she be able to help him in and out without hurting him?

After a final swipe of the dishcloth over the counter, she hustled to the front hall closet for her jacket. Then she nestled Parker into the car seat, ignoring his protests at being separated from the toy. He arched his back and fussed as she clicked the straps into place.

"I know, baby." Grabbing the diaper bag and her purse, she tensed at his increasing cries and lifted the carrier as her cell phone rang.

"Hello?"

"Celeste? This is Sue Roper from Rock of Ages church."

Brandy's old church. Dread pooled in Celeste's stomach.

"Yes, hello, Sue."

"I know you're raising Parker now, and I wasn't sure if you were aware that Brandy's grandmother, Pearl, recently moved to an assisted living facility."

"Yes, I know. I've been meaning to visit." Grandma Pearl. The woman had hosted countless tea parties in her parlor for Celeste and Brandy when they were little girls. Rheumatoid arthritis and weak bones had forced her into an apartment in assisted living. Guilt pinched Celeste. She hadn't visited the endearing lady in a while. At least her parents had brought Parker to see her a few times.

"She would love that," Sue said. "But that's not why I'm calling. We're preparing the children's Christmas Eve program, and we have a favor to ask."

Parker's cries became wails. A favor? She rocked the carrier. "Is there any way I can call you back?"

"It will only take a minute."

"Okay, just give me a second." Celeste suppressed a

sigh and took Parker out of the car seat, settling him in her arms. His cries stopped instantly. "Okay, I'm ready."

"Well, Pearl is very near and dear to us, so the ladies and I have been discussing it, and we want to give her a Christmas surprise. Since Brandy died, she's been really down. Still comes to church, thankfully. Lou Bonner brings her each Sunday. The one thing that brightens her up is Parker. She always talks about him and shows us the pictures you send her."

Celeste's chest tightened. She should be doing more for Grandma Pearl than sending a few pictures now and then.

Sue continued. "Wouldn't she love it if Parker was baby Jesus in the program? I can't think of another gift that would make her happier. I know he's a bit old for the part, but we'd love to have him for Pearl's sake."

In her head, Celeste instantly ticked off problems with the scenario. Parker wasn't walking, but he was at a stage where he hated to be constrained. Having him in a Christmas program seemed overly ambitious. Then there was the fact Grandma Pearl went to Brandy's old church.

There would be questions. And attention. The kind she avoided.

Sure, Sue was friendly on the phone, but what about Brandy's other friends from church? Did they consider Celeste responsible for Brandy's death?

Why wouldn't they? She was the one who'd been driving.

"Um, he doesn't sit all that well right now."

"If he won't sit still, he can be a sheep."

She longed to decline, but this was for Grandma Pearl, and the woman was alone and, most likely, sad. Not to mention Brandy would have wanted Parker in the Christmas Eve program—she'd climb Mount Everest for her beloved grandmother.

"What would I have to do?" Parker tried to wriggle out of her grasp, but she held tight, pretending to blow him kisses. Anything to avoid a meltdown.

"Practices are Thursday nights starting after Thanksgiving. We'll walk the children through their parts and fit them for their costumes. I know it's a lot to ask, but we don't know how many Christmases Pearl has left. Would you do this for her?"

"Of course."

"Thank you. We'll see you in a few weeks."

Celeste hung up with mixed feelings. Maybe Mom and Dad would take Parker to the practices. If not, she would act like an adult, drive him there herself and deal with it.

Wait. The church was on the same road as the accident site. If she drove Parker, she would have to pass the ditch, field and telephone pole where she'd lost so much.

The moments before the car spun out came back. The loud Christmas music, the laughter—what had they been laughing about?—the happy, girls'-night-out feeling she always got when she was with Brandy.

She would never have it again.

Her stomach felt hollow. Mom and Dad would have to drive Parker, because she wasn't ready to confront her past.

There wasn't time to think about it now. She was late. Once again, she strapped Parker into the carrier. He whimpered, rubbing his eyes. She rushed down the porch steps into the rain, slid open the side door of her red minivan and locked Parker's seat into the base before driving the short distance to Sam's. Tossing her hood up to protect her head from the rain, she ascended the kitchen steps and knocked.

"I'll meet you at the bottom of the ramp," Sam yelled.

"Okay." She hurried down the staircase and wiped her palms on her jeans, holding her breath when he rolled her way. "Do you need me to help?"

"No. Got it."

As soon as he reached the passenger side, she held out her hand to help him into the van. He kept his weight on his left leg and got into the seat slowly and with concentrated effort. Parker had finally stopped crying. *So far, so good.*

"Let me put this in the trunk, and we'll be on our way." She clutched the hood together under her chin before awkwardly loading the chair in the back. Once inside the van, she checked on Parker, whose eyelids were heavy, and buckled her seat belt. "Sorry I'm late. Something unexpected came up."

"For a minute, I thought you stood me up."

Stand him up? Not in a million years.

"No, nothing like that. A lady from Brandy's church called."

"Is everything okay?"

"Yeah...well, no. Not really." She shook her head, swallowing the knot in her throat. "Never mind. I don't know what to think. They want to surprise Brandy's grandma by having Parker be baby Jesus in the Christmas Eve service."

"Why do you sound upset? Don't you like her grandma?"

"I love her. She's sweetness personified. In fact, I feel guilty I haven't visited her in a while. She adores Parker."

"Don't feel guilty. You're doing the best you can."

The road wound through trees. The wipers swished rapidly as she sneaked a peek over at Sam's profile. She guessed he smiled a lot—or used to, anyway—by the faint creases around his blue eyes. Did her heart just flutter? He was so handsome, even if he was worried. The lines in his forehead and slight bulge in the vein near his temple didn't lie.

"Are you nervous about today?" she asked.

"Yeah." Sam faced her, and her stomach dipped. *My, oh my.*

She turned and continued along the two-lane road. The forest gave way to farm fields, some with faded yellow cornstalks standing limp in the rain, others with dried stumps of harvested crops. The trees in the distance looked like a watercolor painting of fall colors.

"What else is going on?" The way he said it gave her the impression he'd welcome a distraction.

"I'm still not sure about this baby Jesus thing in the Christmas Eve program."

"He's pretty young." Sam frowned, looking back at Parker. She checked her rearview. He'd fallen asleep.

"Yes, but if he won't cooperate, they'll let him be a sheep."

"Cute." The corner of his mouth kicked up in a grin, and his eyes twinkled. "I'd like to see that."

"Yeah."

"Don't sound so excited."

"I'm not a hundred percent sold on the idea."

"Why not?"

"Well, like you said, he's pretty young. Not even walking yet. And I would have to take him to practices."

"What's so bad about that?" He shifted, watching her.

Everything. Brandy's friends might blame me. And

then there's my face. She tilted her chin up. "The church is a mile north of where my car spun out last December. I would have to pass it to get to the practices."

He didn't say anything for a while, just stared at the rain splashing on the window. "If it would make it easier, I could go with you."

Celeste sucked in a breath. His offer burrowed into her heart. All her reasons for not taking Parker seemed petty. But reality set in. Then doubt. Sam would see other people's reactions. She didn't want him to think less of her.

"Thank you, but I can always ask my parents to take him."

She could feel his stare but didn't bother looking over. He didn't understand, and she wasn't explaining. She wished she could take him up on his offer. Wished she had met him before her accident, when things were different. When even a tongue-tied girl like her might have had a chance at dating a guy like him.

"You've been working on your upper body strength."

"Every morning your voice echoes in my head, chiding me about working hard and pushing through." Sam's left leg trembled at the exertion of the last hour. His right hip was ready to explode. The pain differed from what he'd been feeling at home, though. He recognized it from all those months he'd worked with Dr. Rachel Stepmeyer. The pain of exertion brought a rush. And hope.

Last time he'd hoped, he'd been let down. How many times had he prayed for complete healing? He'd believed God would heal him, too. He'd memorized the Bible verse about being able to move a mountain with enough faith. His faith hadn't lacked. God hadn't listened to him.

God didn't care.

"The good news is your muscles haven't atrophied. You're weaker, obviously, and you've lost some range of motion, but commit to your sessions and you'll get it back. We have a new muscle stimulation system. It could help with your pain." Dr. Stepmeyer typed something into her tablet. "I want you out of the wheelchair more. I know it's hard, but the crutches will force you to build muscle in your legs."

"Yes, ma'am."

That brought a hint of a smile to her face. She handed him a brochure about muscle stimulation. "Read this over and let me know if you want to try it."

"I will." He tucked it between his thigh and the side of the wheelchair.

"See you on Wednesday."

"Thanks."

"Oh, and Sam?"

He waited.

"It's good to have you back."

Nodding, he spun the chair and wheeled away. Rain still pounded against the glass door. He didn't see Celeste's minivan, so he waited near the entrance. Ever since his last doctor's appointment a few months ago, he'd pushed aside the nagging worry that the fall in the shower had killed his chances at ever walking unassisted. After the last surgery, Dr. Curtis had warned him it might take two more years for him to heal. If he healed...

But today Dr. Stepmeyer had assured him he just needed to keep working at it.

His thoughts turned to the conversation earlier in the

car. Sam had made the offer to accompany Celeste to the practices because he thought she needed a friend. And, if he was honest, because he'd been thinking about her more and more each day. He wanted to spend time with her. Enjoyed talking to her. She didn't put pressure on him the way his family did.

The fact she was avoiding the site of her accident didn't surprise him. What did? How quickly she turned him down.

He wasn't used to women turning him down.

Celeste's red minivan stopped at the sidewalk. He pressed the button for the doors to automatically open. The handicap buttons were getting old. His life was getting old.

Would Celeste have said yes if he wasn't in a wheelchair?

He didn't know. He wasn't sure he wanted to find out.

Chapter Three

Celeste pushed the dust mop across Sam's living room floor while Parker stood, knees bouncing as he held on to the wooden coffee table. For three weeks she and Sam had been settling into a comfortable routine, one with clear expectations. She took Sam to and from physical therapy three days a week, shopped for his groceries at the crack of dawn on Tuesday mornings and cleaned on Fridays after his physical therapy session. Sometimes she wished their relationship wasn't so businesslike.

Her mind wandered to her clients' long to-do list waiting at home. She was a virtual assistant to busy, successful people, and working while raising Parker was proving more challenging than she'd expected. To fit in all the projects—from emails and phone calls to invoicing—she got up at six, worked a few hours and did the bulk of her duties when Parker napped or after he went to bed.

Then there was her main charge, Sam. At least she'd managed to nip her growing attraction to him in the bud by telling herself over and over that he was off-limits. Sam treated her for what she was—the caregiver who lived next door.

She sighed. One more room and she'd be finished

with the light cleaning he required. This place needed some music, preferably upbeat Christmas songs. Hard to believe next week was Thanksgiving already.

"You think today will be the day Parker makes his big move?" Sam swung into the room on his crutches. After his therapy session, he'd disappeared to his bedroom to shower and change. His damp hair looked darker than usual, and his smile made her stop sweeping midstroke.

Look away! He can't help he's gorgeous.

Now that she was around more, she'd taken to studying him—to make sure he was okay. While around six feet tall, he wasn't large. He had muscular arms, but his legs were lean from lack of use. Some days his face faded white and his lips tightened to a thin line. Those days she knew he was in a lot of pain. But today he had a relaxed air about him. He settled into his chair, setting the crutches down as he carefully straightened his leg on the ottoman.

He waved to Parker. "I think he'll start walking on his own this week."

"I hope so. Everything I've read said babies usually walk unassisted by twelve months. His pediatrician told me not to worry, but I can't help it."

Parker made a goo-goo noise and zoomed around the table, not taking his hands off it. He tripped, toppling over on his side.

"Oh!" She lurched forward, but Sam held his hand out.

"Let him be. He'll figure it out."

She paused, waiting for a cry, but Parker pushed himself back up and held on to the table once more. He stared at Sam with a big grin, then took a wobbly step toward him.

"Look at that! He's doing it!" Sam held his arms open

wide, reaching as far as his extended leg would allow him. "Come on over, buddy."

Celeste whipped her phone out of her back pocket, fumbling to enter the passcode. She pressed Video and directed it Parker's way. He stood immobile with his hands in the air, but he hadn't taken a step yet. *Come on, come on, you can do it, little man!*

Parker lifted his chunky leg and promptly fell on his bottom. She exhaled the breath she'd been holding. "Oh, well. He'll do it one of these days."

"Maybe today. You never know." Sam made funny faces at Parker, who laughed and crawled to him, pulling himself to the edge of Sam's chair. Sam picked him up.

At the sight of Parker on Sam's lap, Celeste's heart swelled. He always had a smile for her nephew, often shaking his tiny hand or ruffling the hair on his head, but this was the first time he'd held the boy. The picture they presented? Priceless. But unwanted thoughts surged through her mind. *Josh should be here cradling his son. What if Parker never has a daddy?*

What if she ended up raising Parker alone forever? It was a scenario she knew could come true. What guy would want to raise her nephew and wake up to her scars every morning?

Celeste was it for Parker. Part of her loved being his mom, but the other part worried she'd never be enough. The baby had lost his mom and dad, and he was stuck with his aunt who'd basically become a recluse.

She grabbed the dust mop with more force than necessary and swept the rest of the floor while Sam made funny explosion noises and tickled Parker, who giggled loudly. Outside, the wind blew a few straggling brown leaves across the deck. Winter had arrived. Snow would be coming soon.

"Why don't you take a break, Celeste?"

With a few taps she emptied the dishpan in the trash. She never lingered after cleaning, but then, Sam never asked her to stay, either. What would it hurt? Parker looked so content on his lap she didn't have the heart to tear him away. "Okay."

She took a seat on the leather couch. Crossed one leg over the other. Had no clue what to do next. Parker yawned.

"I noticed you running the other day." Sam tucked him under his arm. Be still her heart. There was something very appealing about Sam holding a child. "Your parents still helping out?"

"Yes. They miss him. They swing by after work a few days a week. They'll be here Sunday, too."

"Good." He didn't seem to know what to say, either. His eyes darted around the room. "I didn't know you ran."

"I haven't as much lately. The days are getting shorter, so my long runs are numbered."

"Oh?" He adjusted his leg, holding Parker firmly. Parker's eyes had grown heavy, and he let out another big yawn.

"It's kind of hard with Parker. I have a jogging stroller, but for me, running is a solitary sport. It's not the same pushing a stroller. I'd rather have my arms moving."

"What about a treadmill?"

She twisted her face, sticking her tongue out. "Yuck. Boring. I'm best outside."

"I take it you've been doing it a long time?"

"Running used to be a big part of my life."

"How's that?"

"Well, let's see." She tapped her finger against her chin and flinched, suddenly remembering the tender spot. "I started running cross-country in seventh grade. I ran varsity all four years of high school. Got a partial college scholarship out of it, too."

"Impressive."

She diverted her attention to her lap. "Running kept me focused, but I didn't give enough thought to life after college. It's probably why I have a degree I'm not using." She let out a self-deprecating laugh.

"Well, that makes two of us. I'm not using mine, either." He frowned. "I think I need to change that." She waited for him to say more on the subject, but he shook his head. "I take it you didn't have dreams of marathons?"

"Oh, I had those, all right. I saw myself as the next Joan Benoit."

"Who is she?" He gave her a pointed stare, his eyes playful.

"An amazing American runner."

He looked suitably impressed. "So what happened?"

She shrugged, brushing a piece of lint from her jeans. "No matter how hard I trained, I wasn't as fast as the top runners. I got injured my junior year of college. I'd had tendinitis and other problems off and on, but the stress fracture took a long time to heal. My college career was a disappointment. I did end up running in a few marathons after college."

"Not anymore?"

"No." Memories flitted to her. The feel of packed earth beneath her feet at all those high school races. Sweat dripping down her back as she pushed herself to stay conditioned on lonely roads during the summer. Lifting weights to get an edge. Being top ten in her district, but not good enough to take the state title. She missed those days.

"You don't mind holding him?" She nodded at Parker, who had fallen asleep in Sam's arms. What would it be like to have a man in her life, a husband to help raise Parker?

"Not at all. My niece Emily used to sleep on my lap, before…well, before I had the second surgery. The family doesn't meet here for Tuesday dinners anymore. In fact, no one comes around as much. I didn't want them to."

"I get it. I pushed people away, too." *And some of them pushed me away.*

The clock on the wall ticked as silence stretched.

"You never told me if your parents are taking Parker to the Christmas program practices."

Celeste wrapped her arms around her waist. "I haven't asked them."

"Why not?" He sounded skeptical.

"It slipped my mind." It hadn't slipped her mind, but every time she considered calling Mom to ask, she balked. Something about the request reeked of desperation.

"Well, I should probably go back." She rose. "Is there anything else you need before I leave?"

"Yes, actually." Sam shifted in his seat, his face distorting as he did. "There is something you can do for me. I want to get out of here."

"Oh, okay." Celeste blinked. "Right now? It's kind of cold out."

Sam groaned. That wasn't what he meant. He didn't exactly know what he was asking.

"No." He inhaled Parker's baby shampoo, fighting the frustration bulging inside him. The accident had taken the use of his leg, but sometimes he thought it had taken his speech, too. Conversation had been easy—his strong suit—before the accident. And now? He might as well be a caveman, grunting and gesturing. "I mean in general. I was wondering if I could go grocery shopping with you."

"Oh." Her face fell as she sat back down. "Sure. No problem."

But the way she slumped said it was a problem. "I don't want to go out in the wheelchair. I don't like being stared at, and I need to build strength in my legs. I'm just… Forget it." He jerked his head to the side. Why did he have to be so dependent?

"Well, if you're trying to avoid stares, I'm probably not the best person to be out with." Her hair had fallen in front of her face, the way it had the first few times he saw her.

"Look, I know I'm asking a lot from you, but I've been hiding away for a long time. If I'm going to have any shot at a somewhat normal life, I have to go back to work. I thought if I start getting used to my crutches in public places, maybe it would be easier. I'm just asking to go with you when you have errands to run. Like when you stop in town for coffee or go to the library— that sort of thing."

"I think that's wonderful, Sam." She tucked her hair behind her ear. "But your family is better suited to take you out."

"They all work. I would have to go with them at the busiest times, and everyone in town would stop and ask a million questions. My legs hurt the worst at night." His forehead tightened, and he could feel his pulse hammering in his temple. He hated begging, but he'd given it a lot of thought over the last couple of weeks. Since he was back in physical therapy, he could see how much he'd been missing. It was as though he'd spent the last months under a dark tent, and the flap had opened, revealing a sunny meadow.

Frown lines deepened above the bridge of Celeste's nose. "I'll have to think about it."

"What's there to think about?" He massaged the back of his neck with his free hand. "I understand I would slow you down, but it can't be that big of an imposition."

"You wouldn't slow me down, and you're no imposition." She wrung her hands together. "It's just...well, I don't go to the coffee shop or the library. I do the grocery shopping as soon as it opens, and I practically sprint through the aisles to get it done as quickly as possible."

Some of the things puzzling him about Celeste finally added up. "You don't want people to see your scars."

Her throat worked as she swallowed. Was that a tear glistening in her eye?

"But you're beautiful."

She gasped, staring wide-eyed at him.

He shrugged. "I barely notice them."

"You're the only one, then. I have a follow-up appointment in December. I want more surgery."

Something in her tone made him pause. In his experience, the doctors told him when he needed more surgery, not the other way around. He didn't want to push the issue, though. He'd already brought a tear.

"Celeste?"

"Yes," she whispered.

"Where do you miss going? You know, the places you took for granted before the accident?"

She gazed at the wall, a faraway look in her eyes. "Well, like I said, running. I'd run for miles whenever I wasn't working. And we had a café I loved going to. I'd buy the latest David McCullough biography and just sit and read, sipping a latte. No one would bother me."

She glowed as she spoke, and he wanted to give it to her—her old life—but he could no more fix hers than he could fix his own.

"With the weather getting colder, you won't run outside anyhow, will you?" He couldn't imagine running when it snowed. He'd never been an exercise fanatic. Played basketball now and then, and that was about it.

"Are you kidding? Of course I run in the winter. Ice and negative windchill are the only things stopping me." She waved. "Well, until Parker came along, that is."

Her words gave him an idea. He didn't know if it would work, but he wasn't about to overanalyze it at this point. "What if I watch Parker for you so you can run?"

"What?" She shook her head. "No. I couldn't ask you to do that."

"I realize I'm not the best babysitter material. But if you brought him over here, there's really not anywhere he could go. It's a big open space for him. And I've got a television. We can watch cartoons."

"But your cabinets aren't babyproofed." She stood, crossing her arms over her chest. "What if he falls or something and you can't get to him?"

"I'm not paralyzed. I get in and out of my wheelchair fine, and you know I've been using my crutches longer each day for the past couple of weeks."

Regret shone in her eyes. "I'm sorry. I didn't mean—"

"No offense taken. I understand. If you're worried about babyproofing, we can empty the cupboards. I never use them." He tightened his hold on Parker, so warm against his chest. He wouldn't mind taking care of the little guy for her, not at all. "How long do your runs last?"

"Thirty minutes to an hour. When I trained for marathons, I did longer runs, but I'm not training now." She began to pace. He liked watching her graceful movements.

"Do you want to?" he asked.

She stopped, turning to him. "Do I want to what?"

"Train for a marathon."

"I don't know. I haven't considered it."

"Why not?"

"Well…" She returned to the couch and gave him a frank look. "My life revolves around Parker. And I'm having a hard time fitting everyday activities and work around him. Even taking a shower has gotten complicated."

He didn't doubt that was true, but he guessed her insecurity about her scars was the bigger problem.

"Let me take him off your hands a few mornings a week so you can fit your runs in."

He could see in her face how tempted she was to take him up on his offer.

"You can drop him off first thing Tuesday morning, and afterward we'll go grocery shopping together. Look, you miss running. I miss work. I want to go to the Friday meetings. I want to inspect the cars on my dealership lot, talk to my employees and sell vehicles to my customers. I miss the reports, the quotas, the rush of meeting our sales goals. I need to get back. I might never walk on both feet again, but I can work. I want to work. But I need to do this, first."

Celeste clasped her hands tightly. She had to say yes. She knew it. How could she deny Sam this? But how could she agree?

He didn't know what he was asking.

"I want to help you, Sam, but there's a reason I don't go to the coffee shop and read anymore, and it has nothing to do with Parker. People don't just stare. They ask questions, and sometimes it hurts."

If she took him with her, he'd see how other people viewed her. He'd said she was beautiful—of all the wonderful things he could say!—but he'd see for himself no one else thought she was pretty.

"Maybe you're wrong. They don't know you, but they know me. If you take me with you, the people we run into might not notice you because it's been so long since *I*'ve been out."

She hadn't thought of that. "Yeah, and then a mom will stroll by with her young kids and one will say, 'Mommy, why does she have all those marks on her face?' It's embarrassing, Sam."

His lips lifted in a grin. "I can handle that if you can handle, 'Look, Marge, isn't that the Sheffield boy? What a shame it's been this long and he's still not walking.'"

She giggled. She didn't mean to, but it came out. "Do people actually say that?"

"I don't know." He waved, his eyes twinkling. "It's been months since I've left the cottage. Come on, Celeste. I've got to get out of here. You take me out of this place a few times each week, and I'll watch Parker on the mornings you want to run. In fact, I'm going to put the cherry on top of this deal. You said your accident anniversary is December 18, right? Let's go to the Christmas parade together. You won't have to be alone, and everyone in Lake Endwell can gawk at both of us. We'll make goofy faces back at them."

She'd never seen this side of him, and she liked it. He was charming, funny, and— Wait. Had he just asked her to go with him to the Christmas parade?

For a split second she felt normal.

How she missed feeling normal.

If she accepted Sam's offer, she wouldn't have to dread the anniversary. She'd been fighting off memories of Brandy nonstop. They'd been having a great time that night. The trunk had been full of Christmas gifts for Parker and her parents. If she had known it would be the last time she'd see Brandy, she would have...

"Come on, say yes." The gleam in Sam's eye reminded her of Brandy's—the way she'd rope Celeste into her schemes. Brandy had been so much fun, and Celeste could almost hear her urging, *"What are you waiting for? He's so cute. Say yes already!"*

"Don't say I didn't warn you," she said. "It might not be fun when you see what I have to deal with."

"You'll be too busy trying to make sure I don't slip and fall on my face to notice what anyone else is doing. I haven't walked with crutches anywhere but here."

"You get around good on those, but we should probably take the wheelchair with us, just in case."

"So is that a yes?" His eyes shone with intensity. A warm, excited feeling spread over her body.

"You meant it about the Christmas parade?"

"I meant it."

"Okay, then. You have a deal."

Chapter Four

Snowflakes chased and teased each other outside Celeste's picture window early Tuesday morning. Steam spiraled from the mug of coffee warming her hand. All weekend she'd coaxed Parker, but he still hadn't taken more than one step on his own.

Today would be a day of baby steps for them all.

Her first early morning run since moving to Lake Endwell.

Sam's first attempt at babysitting Parker.

Their first public outing. To the grocery store.

She took another sip and padded in her fuzzy black slippers to the bedroom. She dug around in her dresser to find leggings, a long-sleeve air-wicking T and the rest of the layers. Why had she agreed to this again?

Anticipation revved her nerves at the thought of jogging in the crisp air under the gentle snowfall, but imagining the rest of the day made her stomach heave. What if Sam took his eyes off Parker, and he got into something dangerous? Choked on a toy, or worse, fell?

Would Sam be able to take care of him?

She tossed all the clothes on the bed and shook her head. She'd watched Sam's strong arms scoop Parker onto his lap and knew firsthand his agility getting in and out of the wheelchair. His right leg didn't bend all the way, but he functioned pretty well. His family had cleared out the bottom cupboards over the weekend, and yesterday, she'd installed a portable baby gate with a swinging door to block the hallway leading to his bathroom and bedrooms. Parker would be safe and sound in the huge open living area.

But…

Dear Father, give Sam everything he needs to protect Parker.

As for her promise to take Parker's new babysitter to the grocery store, maybe it would be better for Sam to see people's reactions now—before she let her attraction bloom. Because every time she thought about him, her heart did a little flip. It wasn't just his looks, although his chiseled jawline had made her forget her whereabouts on more than one occasion. It was how he cared about her nephew, the grit he showed going to physical therapy and the fact he'd asked her to the Christmas parade.

A date!

Well, kind of a date.

Once they got through grocery shopping, who knew what she would call it. Would Sam view her differently after he saw how people reacted to her scars? Would he pity her? Pity, she could probably deal with, but the worst would be disgust—she'd seen it a few times around her hometown before she stopped going out.

Half an hour later, she'd fed Parker and changed him into a pair of jeans and an orange sweatshirt sporting a tiger face. Celeste laced her running shoes, pulled her purple fleece headband over her ears and bundled Parker up in his stocking cap and puffy blue coat. She hoisted him on her hip and slung the diaper bag over her shoulder.

Out in the fresh air, Parker raised his face to the sky and squinted as snowflakes tickled his cheeks. He clapped his hands and laughed.

"It's snow. You like it, don't you?" Celeste hugged him close to her. "Guess what? You get to play with Sam today while I go running."

"Mama!" He looked at her and pointed to the flakes.

Had he just called her Mama? Her heart practically thumped out of her chest as a sinking sensation slid down her throat. Could he call her that? Could he call her Mama?

She wasn't his mama. Brandy was. And Brandy would be here if it wasn't for her.

Celeste had been the one who insisted they go out, that Brandy needed a break, needed some fun. She'd been worried about how listless Brandy had become.

I don't have time to think about it now.

After taking a deep breath to calm her nerves, she kissed Parker's cheek and hurried up the steps leading to Sam's kitchen. She knocked, waited for the go-ahead and entered. Swiping Parker's hat off his head, she stomped her feet free of snow, then quickly took off his coat and set him on the floor. He instantly crawled toward the living room. Sam waited on the couch, his right knee in a black brace under his basketball shorts. The skin on his leg held thick purple scars and rivets where he'd lost tissue. She hadn't seen him with his leg uncovered, and the shock of his injuries took her breath away.

"Hey, buddy, you're hanging out with me this morning." Sam held his arms wide as Parker approached. Using the edge of the couch, Parker stood and bounced until Sam picked him up. Sam grinned at Celeste. "What did you feed him this morning? He's excited."

"Apple-and-cinnamon oatmeal. Breakfast of champions." She dragged her toe back and forth in front of her. Maybe this was a bad idea. She forced herself not to stare at his leg. No wonder he dealt with so much pain.

"What's wrong?" He narrowed his eyes at her. "You worried about me watching the little guy? We'll be fine. I've got you and my aunt Sally on speed dial."

"I know. It's just… I've never left him with anyone but my parents, so I'm a little nervous." She bit the corner of her lip. "Plus, my head's kind of messed up right now. A minute ago, Parker called me Mama."

"And that's a problem?"

She shrugged. "I don't know. I wasn't prepared for it. I guess I thought he'd call me Auntie or something."

"But you're his mom."

"I could never replace Brandy."

"That's not the point." He tightened his hold around a wiggly Parker. "You're going to raise him as your son, and you're the only mother he'll ever know. He should call you Mom."

Put in those terms, her reservations didn't make sense. But they still bothered her.

"I just don't want to take this away from her." She'd already taken enough.

"You wouldn't be. You *are* planning on telling him about his mom and dad, right?"

"Of course!"

"Then what's the problem? He'll know he had parents who loved him but who couldn't raise him, much as they would have liked to. And he'll have a mom who loves him and *can* raise him."

She didn't know how to explain. It felt like a betrayal to Brandy and to Josh.

But Parker couldn't call Brandy Mama. She'd never hear that word from his lips.

Maybe Sam had a point.

"I'll think about it." She avoided eye contact until she cleared her throat. "I'd better take off. Do you need anything? His diaper bag is right there by the couch. He shouldn't need a change. Just watch him. He's been putting things in his mouth, and I don't want him to choke."

"We'll be fine." He grinned, playing peekaboo with Parker. "Take your time."

They would be fine. Wouldn't they?

Once she reached the bottom of his porch steps, she inhaled the brisk air, tipped her chin up, pushed through a few light stretches and surged forward.

She had enough on her mind today without adding the whole mama issue. As her feet hit the gravel, she tried to forget about Brandy and what was happening after the run. The less she thought about the upcoming grocery-shopping trip, the better. Yes, a nice long run would help her forget.

Passing tall, stark trees, she rounded a bend. What were Sam and Parker doing now? She'd forgotten to mention Parker had a tooth coming in. Maybe she should go back and grab the teething ring in the fridge, just to be safe.

Her pace slowed.

They'll be fine.

But the worries kept coming. Something told her nothing could clear her muddy mind, not even a long run through snow-topped pines.

Exactly one hour later, Sam waited next to Celeste's minivan while she took Parker out of his car seat to strap him into the shopping cart. Looking around the packed parking lot of Lake Endwell Grocery and the steady stream of people bustling in and out of the automatic doors, Sam didn't care this was step one toward a more mobile life. He wanted one thing. To go home to the privacy of his cottage.

The snow still fell, but it was melting as soon as it contacted the blacktop, so slush wasn't a factor to worry about. He'd still have to be careful on the crutches, though.

Babysitting—all twenty-four minutes of it—had been fun. After a session of tickling Parker until he howled with laughter, Sam had found a fuzzy stuffed elephant in the diaper bag and, with a low voice, pretended to make it talk to Parker. Celeste had chosen that moment to return. Her flushed cheeks had done something funny to his brain, causing him to drop the elephant. Parker had flopped forward trying to get it, forcing Sam to clutch Parker to prevent him from falling. It had been difficult to keep his hold on the baby.

For the first time, he'd seriously doubted his abilities to take care of the boy.

Celeste must not have noticed he'd almost let Parker slip from his hands. All the way here, she'd been chattering nonstop about how great it felt to get outside and clear her head. He couldn't admit he was nervous about watching Parker, not after seeing how happy running made her.

"Are you ready?" Worry lines dug between Celeste's eyebrows. Her hands were encased with black suede gloves, but he guessed her knuckles were white under them. He didn't want to stress her out more by admitting he was nervous. She looked nervous, too.

"Yep." He swung forward. *Watch the puddle. You've got this.*

"It looks busy. We can come back another time if you want."

"Nope. Let's go in."

With a loud breath, she pushed the cart to the entrance.

He stayed by her side, carefully placing each crutch before swinging forward. What would it be like to be shopping as a couple, instead of as the result of an agreement? He liked the idea of cooking with Celeste and picking out cookies and snacks for Parker.

He *really* liked the idea of being able to push the cart.

Where was his head at? Had he gotten a concussion recently and not known it? They weren't a couple. Never would be. And Celeste would see why in roughly six seconds, because he recognized almost every person inside this buzzing beehive. They entered the produce section, and Sam girded himself.

The bright, spacious store felt like a football field compared to his cottage, and Christmas music—"Rockin' Around the Christmas Tree"—played over the sound system. He smelled pumpkin pie and fried chicken. Both made him hungry.

"Well, I'll be." Alma Dartman, a woman in her eighties from church, nudged her husband. "Look, Irv, it's little Sam."

"Who?" Irv's hunched back and thick glasses prevented him from seeing far. His hearing aid buzzed, and he yanked it out of his ear. "Blasted nuisance."

"The youngest Sheffield boy." Her voice carried, and she spoke louder. "The one in the accident. Sam."

Sam closed his eyes for a split second. Why didn't she just announce it over the loudspeaker? Then everyone would know he was here, and that, yes, he'd been in an accident. A few people turned to see what Alma was talking about, and before he knew what was happening, Sam had four people in line to ask him questions. His first instinct was to look for Celeste. She hung back.

"You're walking." Ms. James, Lake Endwell High's retired gym teacher, stopped in front of him. After more than thirty years, she still looked like a gym teacher in her black tracksuit and short gray hair. The only thing missing was a whistle hanging from her neck. "Haven't seen you out in a long time, Sheffield. How've you been?"

"Hanging in there."

Ms. James noticed Celeste and nodded at her. "You in the accident, too?"

Celeste ducked her chin and shook her head. A surge of protectiveness had him taking a clumsy step closer to her.

"Oh, sorry. I assumed...the scars...but that's right. Jeremy was in the boat with you. I heard he made a full recovery and is back in Cheboygan." Ms. James hefted the bag of potatoes in her hand. "Well, I've got to motor. Before you get back at it, there's a run on stuffing mix, so if you're here for Thanksgiving staples, you might want to hit aisle five first." She gave him a knowing look, then walked away.

For a moment he thought the questions were over, but he'd forgotten about Alma and Irv. "How are you doing, dear? We haven't seen you in a while, have we, Irv? Why are you still on those crutches?"

If there was ever a time he wished he could disappear, now was the time. "Hi, Mr. and Mrs. Dartman." He wanted to rub the back of his neck, but he didn't dare let go of the crutch. "I've been back in the wheelchair for a few months. Hurt my knee." He tried to smile, but his face felt crumbly, as did his noodle legs. Coming here was a mistake.

"We're praying for you, honey." Alma patted his cheek. "We'll keep praying. And who is this young woman and baby?" Alma clapped her hands and stood in front of Parker, making kissy faces. "Hello, baby."

"This is Celeste Monroe, my new neighbor, and her son, Parker." He smiled at Celeste, but her hair hid half her face from view, and the side he could see was paler than the white bakery bags he could just make out from the corner of his eye. "It was nice to see you, Mrs. Dartman, but we're going to have to keep going. Parker's due for a nap soon."

"Oh, yes, dear. I remember how cranky babies get without a nap." She wiggled two knobby fingers at Parker, smiled and joined Irv, shouting, "He hurt his knee."

"What?"

"His knee…"

Sam moved next to Celeste. "Are you okay? I'm sorry about that."

"I'm fine," she said in a strained voice. "Nothing to be sorry about. How are you holding up? It's nice of her to pray for you."

He hobbled in the direction of the grapes. "It *is* nice of her to pray. Alma Dartman is sweet. Loud, but sweet." He flashed a grin to Celeste, but she glanced away. "What's wrong?"

"Um, I guess being out. It's kind of new for me." She paused to place a bunch of bananas in the cart.

"If it makes you feel better, it's new for me, too."

"It does." The gratitude shining in her eyes slammed into his chest. He'd felt so useless, his life had seemed so pointless until she'd come along. And she was the one who was grateful?

They slowly gathered fruits and vegetables. Sam had to fight his irritation at not being able to select and bag everything himself. If he tried, he would drop a crutch. He couldn't take that chance. So he told Celeste which tomato he wanted and how many apples to buy. As they made their way to the bakery, he sensed her relaxing.

"Should we get something decadent?" He stopped in front of the row of desserts. A line of shoppers waited in front of the bakery counter. Boy, this place was crowded.

"You should definitely get something decadent." She pointed to a Black Forest cake.

The pumpkin pie aroma from earlier hit him full blast. "What are you doing for Thanksgiving, by the way?"

"Parker and I are having dinner with my parents. What about you?"

"Aunt Sally's. It's a tradition. I probably won't stay long."

A cart bumped into Sam's crutch, flipping it out of his hand. His right foot came down hard on the floor. He sucked in a breath at the pain shooting up his leg.

"Oh, no! Sam, are you all right?" Celeste grabbed his arm to steady him.

"Sorry!" A harried-looking mom stopped with a toddler girl by her side and a baby in the cart. "I didn't see you. I'm so sorry."

"It's okay," he said through gritted teeth.

Celeste bent to pick up his crutch and handed it to him. The little girl pointed at Celeste. "What's on her face, Mommy?"

"Shh!" The mom tugged her hand and pushed the cart ahead. "That's not polite."

"But what are those lines?"

The mom's cheeks turned brick red, and she disappeared around the corner, practically dragging the little girl by the hand.

At the stricken expression on Celeste's face, Sam forgot all about the pain in his leg. This trip was turning out to be the disaster they'd both feared.

"Come on." He couldn't help that his tone was harder than a slab of concrete. "We're getting out of here."

Celeste didn't move. The girl's question and the mom's escape defeated her in ways she hadn't anticipated. It was as if she had driven them away by the way she looked.

Sam's pulse throbbed in his neck, and his eyes had turned slate blue. Sharp, like his jawline.

"We're taking a break. Wheel the cart over here." He swung stiffly toward the floral department. She followed him. A small coffee shop with three round tables hid behind the flower displays. She'd never noticed the area before, probably because she hadn't taken the time to look around. Sam carefully took a seat and propped his crutches against the wall.

"I didn't know this was here." Celeste pushed the cart out of the way and hoisted Parker into her arms.

"Would you mind ordering coffees for us? Cream for me, no sugar. I'll hold Parker."

She handed Parker to Sam and ordered the coffees. Minutes later, she set his on the table and popped the cover off her cappuccino. Sam didn't touch his drink, though. Instead, he covered her hand with his. "I'm sorry about back there."

Emotion pressed against the backs of her eyes, but she swallowed her embarrassment. "Don't be. I'm used to it."

"Well, you shouldn't have to be used to it. I'm not. I'm about ready to make a sign that says, 'My leg is not up for conversation.' Why is it the first thing people comment on?"

She blew across the top of her drink. "I don't know. I guess it's human nature."

"It shouldn't be." Sam rapped his knuckles on the table. Parker started fussing and reaching for Sam's coffee. "Sorry, bud, you're too young for this." He gestured to the diaper bag. "Did you bring anything for him?"

She found a baggie of crackers and a sippy cup. Sam handed them to Parker, who took the cup in both hands and leaned back into Sam's chest. Longing pinched her heart. Sam's support tempted her to count on him. But how could she? The past five minutes revealed her new reality. People were uncomfortable around her because of her scars.

Was she partly to blame?

"I wish I handled things better." She took a tentative sip of her drink. Still too hot. "I never know what to say, and I get so self-conscious."

"I'm no help there. The last thing I want to discuss at the grocery store is my leg. It's hard enough getting around on it."

The tension in her neck melted. He felt self-conscious, too. It wasn't just her.

"How is your leg, by the way? Maybe I should take you home."

"Nah, she nailed the crutch, not my leg. I lost my balance, came down hard on my foot. It hurt at first, but it's leveled off." The strain around his mouth told her otherwise.

"Do you need an aspirin or anything?"

"I'll take one at home."

Grocery shopping shouldn't be this complicated. And they'd gotten through only a quarter of the list. She sighed and took another sip of the coffee.

"Well, I think we hit everything we discussed last Friday. The awkward questions. Me almost falling flat on my face. What more can happen? Did we forget something?"

Celeste chuckled. She couldn't help it. "You're right. If someone had been listening in on our conversation, they might have thought we were being melodramatic. But clearly, we knew what we were talking about."

"You can say that again." Sam lifted the cup to his lips, and Celeste let out a teeny sigh. What was it about this man that had her heart tying itself up into knots? He leaned back. "Since we've survived produce—and I use the term *survived* loosely—are you up for heading back to the bakery?"

"I think so, but will it bother you if people stop us and ask more questions?" She couldn't ask what she really worried about. Did it bother him when people pointed out her ugly scars?

"I guess I'll have to get used to it." He tilted his head. "I can't change the fact my leg doesn't work right."

"No, I didn't mean about your leg…" She twisted a napkin, darting her eyes to the side.

"Hey." He reached forward and lifted her chin with his finger. "You're the most beautiful woman here. You can't help that people notice you."

His words seeped into her soul, leaving a splendid emptiness where she'd been storing a full supply of insecurities.

"You're a terrible, wonderful liar, Sam Sheffield. And I love you for it. Thank you."

His face went blank.

"We'd better get back out there before the bakery sells out." Celeste forced a teasing quality to her tone. "There's a Black Forest cake with your name all over it."

Maybe she shouldn't have mentioned love. She'd

meant it casually. He obviously didn't realize she'd said it as a joke.

Or had he guessed the truth? It would take all of three seconds for her to mean it for real.

Chapter Five

"Were you expecting the football team or something, Aunt Sal?" Sam handed the heaping platter of turkey to his sister Libby. Even though he'd had his misgivings about the holiday with his family, it felt good to be back. Getting around Aunt Sally's house on crutches was a welcome change from being alone at home. The best part? His siblings were treating him less as a trauma patient and more as their brother. Maybe he'd stay longer than he'd originally planned.

"What are you talking about, Sam?" Aunt Sally's blond hair was pulled back with an orange headband, and glittery pumpkin earrings dangled from her ears. "Football ended two weeks ago. Too bad varsity didn't make it to the play-offs. Do you need a dinner roll, hon?"

"Already have one."

She widened her eyes at the butter dish in her hand. He nodded, and she passed it over. Aunt Sally had been like a mother to him. He had no memories of his own mom, who died giving birth to Libby when he was two. But between Aunt Sally and his older sister, Claire, he figured he had the mom thing covered.

"So I heard you were at the grocery store this week,

Sam." The twinkle in Libby's eye sent warning flags soaring. "And I heard Celeste and Parker were with you."

Since it wasn't a question, he saw no reason to reply. He shoveled a mound of mashed potatoes into his mouth. He was just glad his foot was okay from the impact of that lady's cart hitting his crutch. He'd iced the leg when he got home, and so far, he suffered no lingering side effects.

"You went to the grocery store?" Claire set her fork down. She sat across the table and to the right of him. "I don't remember the last time you went anywhere other than a doctor's appointment."

Again, no need to reply. He bit into his roll.

"I also heard you weren't in the wheelchair." Libby rested her chin on her fist, and her blue eyes twinkled. "Celeste is clearly a genius."

He fantasized about throwing his napkin on the plate and leaving the table in a huff, but it would take too long to get up with his crutches. Besides, the food was really good.

"Or maybe *you're* the genius," Claire said softly. "Celeste has had a rough time of it. Her mom's friend Nancy told me how difficult it's been for her to go out in public."

"Right. Let's change the subject." He looked to his brothers, Tommy and Bryan, for some backup.

"Who's Celeste?" Tommy asked. His daughter Macy sat next to him, and little Emily was on the lap of his wife, Stephanie.

"Really, Tom?" Stephanie sounded exasperated. "I told you she moved next door."

"The one living in Claire's cottage," Bryan added, giving his wife, Jade, the basket of rolls.

"Oh, that's right," Tommy said. "She's taking care of her nephew. Didn't you say something about her being in an accident, too?"

"Car accident," Claire said.

Sam took a drink of his water as his blood pressure rose. The way they were discussing Celeste irritated him on all levels. "Why is the fact she was in an accident so important? It shouldn't define her." *Or me.*

The table went quiet until Dad spoke up. "Tell us more about her."

He wanted to switch topics, but he'd gotten himself into this. "Celeste ran cross-country in college. She has a degree in history, but since she's raising her nephew, Parker, she prefers to work from home. Her brother died overseas. She's doing a good job as a mom." He stabbed a yam. "Now can we talk about something else?"

She sees more than my injuries. She's nice. She joked the other day that she loved me, and all I could think was I wish it could be true. I wish I could date again and have a future with a woman like Celeste.

"Done." Reed, Claire's husband, stood. "Should we tell them?"

Claire blushed, nodding.

"Sam, you made this easy on me." Reed grinned. "We didn't know how to announce this, so here goes. We're having a baby."

Aunt Sally squealed. Libby's mouth dropped open. Macy started clapping, which caused Emily to start clapping, too. Everyone talked at once.

"Congratulations…"

"When are you due?"

"Boy or girl?"

"How long have you known? Do you have morning sickness?"

Sam wiped his mouth with his napkin. While he was happy for Claire and Reed—they'd been trying for a long time to have a baby—his ribs seemed to be closing in on him. He took a moment to study his huge family around the table, and he couldn't help wondering when it would be his turn. When would something great happen to him?

They all had the ingredients for the life he wanted.

Closing his eyes, he could picture Celeste sitting here and Parker on his lap.

Reality crashed down.

He hadn't worked in over a year. Could barely walk. He'd watched Parker for twenty-four minutes and almost dropped him. He couldn't protect Celeste from insensitive questions. Couldn't protect her from anything. Until he got his life together—if he got his life together—his fantasies would remain unreachable.

Could he get his life together?

The doctors had never wanted him back in the wheelchair after the last surgery, but...

He'd blamed it on the constant pain. Refusing to use the crutches hadn't just been due to pain, though.

He'd given up. On walking, on healing, on working, on living.

Maybe it was time.

Time to take another step.

Thinking about dating again was futile at this point. What was left?

Work. Work he could do. His dealership had been everything to him, and he'd let it slip between his fingers.

Sam caught Bryan's eye and motioned for him to come over.

"What's up?" Bryan knelt next to him.

"After dinner, can we talk about Sheffield Auto?"

"Of course, man."

"I'm going back to work in January." Sam had no idea how, but he had to try. "I'll be at the meeting next Friday."

"That's great." Bryan grinned, clapping him on the back.

The old Sam wouldn't have let anything keep him from making the dealership a success. And he would have asked Celeste out—he'd enjoyed a healthy dating life even if he'd never fallen in love. He might not be ready to date, but he could spend time with Celeste without feeling like an invalid.

Before he lost his courage, he sent Celeste a quick text.

If you're not busy Saturday morning, will you stop by?

"Where did Dad go?" Celeste cleared the final plate from the table. "He's usually first in line for pumpkin pie."

"He's picking up Grandma Pearl. We invited her for dinner, too, but her nephew is eating with her. She sounded excited to come here for dessert, though."

Celeste's emotions played tug-of-war. She wanted to spend time with Grandma Pearl, and in the past, they'd avoided discussing Brandy, but what if the conversation took a bad turn? What if Grandma Pearl asked questions about the accident, questions Celeste didn't know how to answer?

"You didn't tell me how the shopping trip with Sam went. Your first time out together, right?" Mom snapped a lid on the plastic container full of gravy and stacked it on top of the leftover stuffing.

"Yes, it was our first attempt." She tossed the old coffee filter in the trash and filled the pot with fresh water. "It was interesting." She filled her mother in on the stares, the inappropriate questions, the little girl whose face was seared into her brain.

The only thing she wasn't revealing? Sam's words after. The ones she'd memorized and kept coming back to. *You're the most beautiful woman here. They can't help but notice you.* But his reaction to her stupid comment about loving him kept her feet on the ground, where they belonged. She'd spent two days trying to decipher the look on his face.

Horror?

Too dramatic.

Fear?

Maybe.

He might be worried that she was falling for him.

He probably had a right to be worried.

"I'm sorry." Mom hugged her, then stepped back, looking her in the eye. "What did you say to the little girl?"

"Nothing. I froze. I…just don't know how to handle those situations."

"Hmm…"

The coffeemaker made gurgling noises as the pot began to fill.

"Would you feel better if you had a reply ready when someone asks about your face?"

"Oh, I have a reply ready, all right." Celeste crossed her arms over her chest and jutted her chin out.

Mom laughed. "I'm sure you do, but I was thinking more along the lines of something nice."

"You got me there." She grinned. "I have no idea how to respond. It's so embarrassing."

They went back to the living room.

"Kids say the first thing in their heads. They don't realize they're hurting your feelings."

"I know." Celeste sat on the couch and hugged a throw pillow to her chest. "The mom's face said it all— she was probably more mortified than I was."

"Exactly. And you're most likely going to have to deal with this again."

"Undoubtedly."

"How would you feel if you said something simple like, 'I was in a bad car accident'?"

The familiar sensation of floundering churned her insides. "Would I have to give details?" Because the details were there, and they haunted her. One minute happy. The next minute waking up after surgery, unable to see because both eyes had puffed shut. She couldn't talk. Her tongue had swollen, she'd lost a tooth, and her nose had been broken.

Blind, mute and confused.

She hadn't known where she was or what had happened. When the nurses told her she'd been in an accident, all she could think was she had to see Brandy.

Mom had broken the news to her.

And if she could have wept, she would have. But she'd lain there, immobile, hooked to a million tubes, afraid she'd never see again. She'd wanted to die. She'd already lost Josh that year. Life without Brandy hadn't seemed possible. Still didn't seem possible.

"Honey, are you okay?" Mom asked.

"Yeah." She shook her head free of the memories. "Why?"

"You didn't answer my question."

"Sorry, got lost in my own little world." She propped her elbow on the arm of the couch and let her cheek rest against her palm. "What did you ask?"

"I asked what you would feel comfortable telling a stranger."

"The truth. Like you said, I was in a bad car accident." It seemed easy...if it worked. "What if they ask more questions?"

"Just because they ask doesn't mean you have to answer. You could say you're thankful to be alive and leave it at that."

The front door opened and Dad hollered, "Hope you have the pie cut because we're ready for dessert."

Celeste's nerve endings prickled. She hadn't seen Grandma Pearl in a long time. She stood to greet her as she emerged from the hall. Grandma Pearl still had silver hair and the kindest eyes in the world, but she walked with a stoop, and her thin face looked sallow.

"Celeste!"

Celeste gave her a big hug. "Happy Thanksgiving. We're so glad you came."

"Got my hair done yesterday." Grandma Pearl pretended to fluff the back. "It's not every day I have dessert with my great-grandbaby."

"Want me to wake him? He's taking a nap. The excitement wore him out."

"Let him sleep a bit more." Grandma Pearl sat at the dining table, and Celeste helped her mom get out plates and mugs. After pouring coffee, they all dug into pumpkin pie.

"How have you been feeling?" Celeste asked.

"Tired and creaky, but I'm doing well." Grandma Pearl's coffee cup trembled as she lifted it to her mouth. "Tell me about your new home. Your dad said you're living over in Lake Endwell now."

"Yes. Parker and I have a beautiful view of the lake.

He's almost walking on his own. We keep waiting for him to take more than one step."

"We?"

Celeste's cheeks flamed. "My neighbor Sam and me. He's the one I'm helping out in exchange for the cabin. He was in a bad accident, too."

Grandma Pearl cut a bite of pie with her fork. "I'm sorry to hear that. It broke my heart the day I got the call about you and Brandy. She shouldn't have died so young." She pulled a handkerchief from her pocket and dabbed under her eyes. "Tragic. But I hope you know I'm thankful every day you survived, dear."

Celeste bowed her head. *It should have been me. Brandy should be here eating pie with her grandma.*

"What would we have done without both you girls? And what would have happened to sweet Parker." She smiled at Mom and Dad. "I know you two would have raised him, but it's better for him to have a young mom like our Celeste."

Celeste clutched her hands together tightly. *Brandy had a son who needed her—still needs her. I need her. And I'm single. Why her? Why not me? The world could have gone on fine without me.*

Parker yelled "Mama" from the bedroom. Another thing Celeste was torn about.

"I'll be right back." She hurried down the hall. Parker stood in his portable crib and lifted his arms. "Mama!"

She picked him up, pressing him close to her. He smelled so baby fresh. She took a minute to savor his warm, cuddly arms around her neck. Was it wrong to love this child so much? "Guess what? Grandma Pearl is here. She can't wait to see you."

He scrunched his nose and patted her cheeks.

"I love you, Parker Monroe."

"La!"

She kissed him and carried him back to the table.

"There he is!" Grandma Pearl clapped her hands and held her arms wide. Parker wiggled to get out of Celeste's grasp. She set him on his feet. He grinned and laughed. Took one step. Two steps. Three…and he was in Grandma Pearl's arms.

"He did it! He walked!" Mom jumped out of her chair and clapped. "Good job, Parker."

Celeste ran to the kitchen to get her phone, but by the time she got back, Grandma Pearl had already set him on her lap and was feeding him a bite of pie.

"We didn't get it on video." Dad sounded disappointed.

"We'll get the next one." Celeste winked. She noticed a text from Sam.

He wanted her to stop by on Saturday? A warm feeling radiated all the way up from her toes to her head. She quickly texted back that she'd stop by around nine Saturday morning.

"This is the best Thanksgiving I could have asked for." Grandma Pearl beamed.

It seemed fitting Parker would take his first steps into Grandma Pearl's arms. A gift to her when she'd lost so much. God was good. Even in the hardest parts of life, God was good.

Grandma Pearl deserved some good in her life.

Celeste would have to keep reminding herself how much Parker meant to the woman. Because the Christmas program practices started in exactly one week. And she was not ready to drive past the accident site.

She wasn't ready to discuss the accident with Brandy's church friends, either. Mom made a good point about having an answer ready for curious strangers. But for the people who knew Brandy? The ones who might have questioned Celeste's driving that night?

She had no answers for them. None at all.

Mom and Dad had assured her over and over it was an accident and how thankful they were she'd made it out alive. But it didn't change the fact that Celeste was here eating pie with Brandy's grandma and raising Brandy's son when Brandy should be the one doing both.

I'm sorry, God. I'm sorry I love Parker so much and I'm happy he's mine. I shouldn't be happy about it, should I? How can I let him call me Mama? It's selfish. I'm selfish.

The emotional turmoil swirled inside her. Only one person came to mind who might understand.

Sam.

The startled look on his face when she jokingly said she loved him crashed back.

Her current strategy of staying silent on the subject of Brandy's death seemed wise, but her heart ached to spill everything to Sam.

Sam zipped his winter jacket Saturday morning and hoped this outing would help him feel less like an invalid and more like a man. He was glad Celeste had agreed to join him. The weather was cooperating. Clear sky and sunshine.

"You're bundled up." Celeste entered by the kitchen door, followed by a chilly breeze.

She and Parker wore winter coats and matching green-and-white knit hats. She looked young and free, less somber than she often did. Sam stared a moment too long. Had the craziest urge to take her hand in his.

Yeah, that would go great. Instead, he shoved a black hat on his head.

"Hey, buddy." Keeping hold of his crutches, he gave Parker a little wave. "Ready for a walk?"

Celeste's mouth dropped open.

Sam quickly added, "Outside. The three of us."

"Are you sure?" The look she gave him screamed, *You're crazy, right?*

"Do you know how long it's been since I've spent any time outside? I'm just talking about a short walk by the lake." He waited, ready to argue whatever problem she dished out. It had taken him thirty minutes to layer jeans over his knee brace and don the rest of his outdoor gear along with running shoes. He was not backing out now.

"I'll go get the stroller."

He nodded. "I'll meet you in the driveway."

Holding Parker, she left with a soft click of the door behind her.

That went better than he'd expected. His sisters would have lectured him about not taking chances, and he would have argued with them until his face turned as blue as the sky above.

He positioned himself in the wheelchair and wedged his crutches upright between his legs as he wheeled out to the patio, down the ramp to the driveway. The air smelled crisp, the way only a forty-degree day on the lake could smell. It hadn't frozen yet, and the water looked turquoise. Sam sucked in a deep breath, lifting his face at the pleasure of it.

He'd just gotten to his feet when Celeste returned. The jogging stroller crushed the gravel as Parker pounded his hands on the bar.

"I'll put the wheelchair under the deck to protect it." She

jammed her foot on the stroller brake, moved the wheelchair and was back in a flash. "Where are we going?"

"This way." He jerked his head to the lake. "Let's
take the path."

They fell in beside each other as geese honked over-
head. Trees rustled in the breeze, and a quiet peace
spread over the lake. Sam soaked it all in. He'd missed
this aspect of life—the simple pleasure of a stroll outdoors on a winter day. "I forgot how quiet this time of
year is when you're outside."

"I never thought about it, but you're right. No bugs
buzzing about, I guess."

"And the trees lost most of their leaves, so they're
quieter, too."

They continued past her cottage.

"How was your Thanksgiving?" they asked simulta-
neously. Sam grinned, and Celeste laughed.

"You first," he said.

"Really good. Dad deep-fried the turkey. It was deli-
cious. Brandy's grandma came over for dessert— Oh!
I forgot to tell you! Parker finally walked—right into
her arms. It was amazing."

"He did? And here I'd been hoping I'd get to see it.
Well, good for you, buddy." He stretched his neck to
make a funny face at Parker. He had been hoping to
see his first steps. Could he be getting too emotionally
invested in his neighbors?

He looked around at the grass starting to yellow, at
the evergreens and the glints of light sparking from the
water. Maybe it was okay to be emotionally invested.
He wouldn't be out here today enjoying this beauty if
it wasn't for Celeste moving in next door.

"What about your Thanksgiving? Your aunt's house,
right?"

"It was good. Really good. My family treated me like a normal human being for the first time in a long time. Oh, and Claire and Reed are having a baby, so I'll be an uncle again." He grinned, but his heart fell. He loved being an uncle, but would he ever be a father?

"That's wonderful!" Celeste beamed.

"Ga! Ga!" Parker pulled himself forward and pointed. Sam stared in the direction he was pointing.

"Look, he found a cat."

A fat orange cat sat facing the lake. Its fur was fluffed up, making it look like a puffball.

"Do you think it's cold?" Celeste asked.

"Doubt it. Looks pretty happy to me. It's definitely being fed."

"You can say that again." She chuckled. "It's got to be twenty pounds. Someone may be feeding it too much."

"Like my aunt Sally. She had enough food at Thanksgiving to feed a small country. Not that I'm complaining. She's a fantastic cook."

"Well, congratulations about Claire having a baby. They must be excited."

"Yeah, it's taken them a while to get pregnant, so they're happy."

They passed the cat, and Parker twisted to try to see it before giving up and settling back in the stroller.

"I remember when Brandy found out she was having Parker." Celeste smiled, a faraway look in her brown eyes. Sam forced his gaze back on the path. He'd never felt this comfortable around a woman he was attracted to, but Celeste was easy to be with. She shook her head. "She flipped out. Took four tests. We jumped up and down in her tiny living room, laughing and screaming. Then we got ice cream."

"You must miss her."

Celeste nodded, the light in her eyes dimming. "I've been struggling with it more lately. I'd begun to make peace with losing Josh and then…"

"You lost *her*."

"Yeah." She slowed the stroller and turned to him. "It's not just missing her. This is probably going to sound stupid, but sometimes I feel like an impostor, like I shouldn't be raising Parker. She should be here raising him."

Sam frowned, trying to take in what she was saying. "But she's not here. Who else would love him the way you do?"

"True. Is it wrong to love him so much, though? I'm fighting these weird feelings. I don't know what's wrong with me."

He paused, resting on the crutches. "Nothing is wrong with you. You're raising a kid, and it's not as if you have any experience. Plus, you miss your friend, and you don't have a husband to help you. I'd be wrestling with a lot of thoughts, too."

She blinked, her lips twisting. "So you don't think I'm betraying her memory or anything?"

"You'd be betraying her memory if you didn't love Parker as your own son. Isn't that what she would want? For him to be raised in a home full of love?"

She nodded.

"I never knew my mom. I was two when she died giving birth to Libby." He gestured for them to continue forward. "My dad raised me."

"I didn't know that. I'm so sorry." They reached a section canopied by trees.

"Don't be. My aunt Sally and my sister Claire were all the motherly figures I needed in my life. Do I wish I'd had my mom? Of course. But I turned out fine, and

I'm grateful for the family I have. They annoy me at times, but I still love 'em."

"I understand." She grew serious. "I've never seen you out here. Why did you decide to come out today?"

It was his turn to grow serious. "I told Bryan I'm returning to work in January."

"That's wonderful, Sam. When did you decide this?"

"Thanksgiving. I guess I'm reclaiming my life little by little."

"Are you nervous about the pain? I know you didn't want to use your wheelchair at work, but if you're going back so soon, I guess you'll have to, huh?"

No way was he working in the wheelchair. "My physical therapist wants me on crutches."

"Oh." The wind blew her hair across the front of her face and neck. "I hope you'll take it slow. Don't want you aching and miserable."

She didn't think he could handle it. Would she always see him as the patient next door?

The temptation to pray—to ask God for help—hit him.

Like God would waste time helping him now, when He'd ignored Sam's pleas all last year.

Sam would do this on his own.

So far, the longest he'd been on his feet with the crutches was two hours, and his knee had felt as if a fireworks display was exploding inside it afterward. Eight to ten hours on crutches were sure to be grueling. Or impossible.

He increased his pace, flinching when his crutch hit a stone. *Slow down. Do you want your knee to blow out again?*

"Well, I'll be happy to drive you Friday," Celeste said. "You don't mind?"

"Of course not." She frowned.

"What's wrong?"

"I just remembered Thursday night is the Christmas Eve program practice."

"That's right." From the look on her face, he'd say she dreaded it. "I'm going with you."

"You don't have to—"

"I'm going. I know you're worried about it. You've done a lot for me. Let me do this for you."

Her shy smile sent a zip of pride down to his toes. Maybe she was starting to see him as more than a patient. He wanted to be there for her, to be the friend she needed. Most of all, he didn't want to let her down.

Chapter Six

"I can't go back to the cottage. Not yet," Sam said, eyeing Celeste's parked van as they came out of the diner on Main Street Monday afternoon. His physical therapy session that morning had gone so well he'd asked Celeste and Parker to join him for lunch—his treat. Although the place had been packed with customers, only a handful of people had stopped by their table asking him how he was. The waitress stared overly long at Celeste, but mostly, they'd eaten in peace. He didn't want the peace to end. Not yet. "What a perfect winter day."

"Where do you want to go?" Celeste carried Parker, who clapped his mittened hands, his face full of joy at being outside.

Snow had fallen the night before, giving the lampposts and trees a frosted look. The sun made everything sparkle, and the Christmas decorations throughout town added to the season's cheer.

"How about a little window-shopping?" He spied the town Christmas tree a few blocks down. He'd skipped Christmas last year. And before that? He'd taken it for granted. "I know you have to get back to work, but it's been a long time since I've hung out down here."

"I don't mind. Should I get the stroller?"

"How wiggly is he?"

Parker bounced in her arms. She chuckled. "I'll get the stroller."

A few minutes later, Sam led the way down the sidewalk, pointing out stores as they passed. "My best friend, Jeremy, and I used to spend all our allowances in there." He stopped before a drugstore/gift shop. "They had a huge selection of candy. You could buy caramels, chocolates, taffy and hard candies in bulk."

"Do they still sell bulk candy?" Celeste stretched her neck to see inside the window.

"I don't think so."

"Want to find out?"

He was taken aback, surprised she suggested it. But she hadn't flinched at eating lunch with him earlier, so maybe she was getting used to being out in public the same way he was.

"Yeah. Let's go in. If they still have the candy, I'm buying a bag."

"Fair enough." She bent to lift Parker from the stroller. He babbled all the way inside. An employee barely glanced up from behind the checkout counter, and a pair of women perused the greeting cards.

"The candy bins used to be here." He went to the back wall where shelves of cough syrups and allergy medicines were placed. "There was a hanging scale, too, so you could weigh your candy before buying it."

"You bought a lot of sweets, didn't you?" She set Parker on the floor, keeping a tight hold on his little hand.

"You have no idea." He leaned against his crutches and smiled at the memories of running in here as a kid to blow his allowance. "I'm pretty sure I single-handedly kept our dentist in business."

She chuckled. "Brandy and I rode bikes all summer from the time we were twelve until we could drive. We ate our fair share of candy, too. And ice cream." Parker reached for a small stuffed bunny. "No, sweetie, that's not for you to touch." She steered him away from the display, and his light brown eyes filled with tears.

"I'll buy it for him." Sam smiled at Parker.

Celeste's eyes shone but she shook her head. "I appreciate it, Sam, but I don't want him expecting a toy every time we go to a store."

He almost argued, but Parker had already forgotten about the stuffed animal and was pulling Celeste to the colorful candy bars in his sight. "So you have a sweet tooth, too, huh?"

"Mine is more of a salty tooth. I can pack away a bag of chips. But I won't turn down a candy bar, either."

"Chips should be their own food group." After Sam purchased three candy bars and a pack of gum, they exited the store, and once Celeste strapped Parker back into the stroller, they continued down the sidewalk. They stopped in a few more stores before strolling to the town Christmas tree. It stood at the entrance to City Park with the white pillars of the gazebo visible behind it. Snow dripped from the branches, which were covered in lights.

"It's so pretty." Celeste stretched her neck back to see the star on top. "Look, Parker, isn't it the biggest Christmas tree you've ever seen?" He held his arms up for her to unstrap him. She glanced at Sam. "Do you want to stay a minute or head back?"

"Stay." He lowered himself onto one of the benches facing the tree as she set Parker on his feet, adjusting his hat and mittens. Parker giggled, slapping the bench seat over and over with both hands. "Doesn't take much for you to have fun, does it, buddy?"

"Mind if I take a picture?" Celeste's brown eyes waited for an answer, but she was so pretty he forgot the question. She cocked her head to the side. "Sam?"

"What?" He tore his gaze away and held out his hand for Parker to take. Parker patted it.

"I want to take a picture. He looks so cute in his snow boots."

"Sure." Sam got Parker's attention, pointing for him to smile at Celeste. "Hey, there, look that way."

The boy laughed, his eyes glued to Sam, and placed both hands on Sam's thigh.

"Guess I'll have to be in it, too." Sam turned Parker to face Celeste. "Say 'cheese.'"

Parker squealed in delight as Celeste snapped the photo.

"Why don't you let me take a picture of you with him?"

"That's okay." She ducked her chin. "I should probably get back. I have a long list of work to do."

"Come on, let's get a photo of you two." He wanted to hold on to today. It had been so long since he'd enjoyed being out. He'd like to look back at this moment and remember Celeste's smile and Parker's happiness. Capture the joy of the moment. Didn't Celeste feel it, too?

"No." Her clipped voice set him back.

"Okay." He got to his feet as she took care of Parker. Why did he keep forgetting about her scars? "Do you ever take pictures of you two together?"

She didn't answer, but her nose twitched.

"Celeste, don't you think he'll want to look back at you and him?"

"Not like this."

They headed back to her van in silence, and he couldn't

help feeling he'd messed up their friendship. If she could see herself the way he did—glowing, smiling—a person he wanted to spend time with. But she clearly didn't see herself that way.

He didn't know how to fix it. He didn't even know how to try.

Celeste's fingertips tapped against the keyboard as she finished typing an ad for a new client. She needed to cram three hours of work into the twenty minutes she had left before driving Parker to the Christmas program practice. What she wouldn't do to call Sue Roper and cancel tonight. The sour taste on her tongue grew positively pungent. She popped a peppermint candy in her mouth.

They were counting on her. A Christmas surprise for Grandma Pearl.

She'd floor it past the accident site if she had to, but she would get Parker to the rehearsal.

The calendar hanging on the bulletin board above her desk caught her eye. Bright green X's showed the countdown. Today was December 2, just two weeks—a mere fourteen days—until her follow-up appointment. An appointment that could free her of these chains. Too ashamed to have her picture taken, even with sweet Parker. How sad was that? And what did Sam think about it? His comment Monday about Parker wanting to look back at pictures of them had dented her ironclad stance about not drawing attention to her face.

Earlier, she'd forced herself to do a little research about becoming a teacher. She glanced at the blue folder with the information she'd gathered. All the steps she needed to pursue a career teaching history. Right in there. She'd have to take almost a dozen college courses, which she could do online, and once done, she could sign up for student teaching and begin the process of getting state-certified. It would take at least two years, maybe more, before she could even think about teaching.

But could she really consider it?

It depended on her plastic surgeon.

Was she wrong to pause her life until she got the outcome she longed for?

Focus. She didn't have time for dreaming.

After a quick scan of the ad, she printed a copy to proofread later. Then she marked the item off her checklist and went to the next one.

Six in the evening and already pitch-black out. Maybe the darkness would make it easier... She wouldn't have to see the crash site when she drove past. But she'd still have to interact with the people from Brandy's church, many of whom had known Brandy and also had small children.

Celeste had no idea how she'd be received by them.

At least Sam was driving with her tonight. They'd survived another round of grocery shopping Tuesday, this time with only two locals stopping Sam about his leg, and, thankfully, nobody said a word about her scars. She'd actually enjoyed the trip. It helped that since Monday, Sam had gone out of his way to keep things light. She was learning more about him.

He ate mostly healthy foods, and he knew all kinds of fun facts. He'd explained how to figure out if a pineapple was ripe by plucking an inner leaf out of the top. If it came out easily, the pineapple was ready. Who would have known? Most of the food he bought was portable and easy to grab. Single-sized yogurts, sliced cheese, lunch meat, crackers, granola bars. He explained that with both hands on the crutches, it was difficult to carry anything. That was why he kept a bag he could sling over his shoulder at all times to carry things between rooms.

She learned more than his food preferences, though. He was funny, kind. He treated her like a trusted friend. What a gift to have his friendship.

A text came through from Sam. We'd better leave early. It's starting to snow.

Tiny white pellets blew past the window. With a frustrated exhalation, she saved her work, got up from the desk and stretched both arms over her head.

Lord, You've gotten me through some big changes lately. I need Your help tonight. Give me the strength to drive to church and the words to say when we arrive.

She'd put more thought into her mom's suggestion. She'd keep any replies to questions about her face simple and direct. No lengthy explanations—assuming she could will her mouth to open and speak at all.

Ten minutes later Parker was babbling quietly in his car seat while Celeste helped Sam into the passenger side of her van.

"You ready for this?" Sam asked as she pulled away.

"As ready as I'm ever going to be." She licked her chapped lips and headed north. The church was twenty-five minutes away. That left about twenty-four minutes before they passed the dreaded spot. In the meantime, she needed a distraction. Sam. "What about you? Ready for the big meeting tomorrow?"

She peeked over to catch his reaction. His hair was expertly gelled on top, and although it was dark, she could make out the twinkle in his eyes as he nodded.

Yep, he was a good distraction. A good, gorgeous distraction.

"I'm ready, thanks to you. I'm not as worried about slipping and falling with the crutches, and I forced myself to walk around the house with them for three hours."

"You won't be marching around on those through the dealership tomorrow, will you?"

"No. But come January, I will be. I've got to be prepared. My job has never really been a desk job. I spend a lot of time checking the different departments, talking to customers and inspecting the lot."

"It's great to hear you excited." Celeste flipped on the wipers as the snowfall increased.

"Do I sound excited?" he joked. "I'm nervous."

"Why?" She glanced at him. "You'll be fine."

He rubbed his chin and shrugged. "Been a long time."

"It'll all come back to you."

"That's what I'm afraid of."

She chewed on the comment a minute. She understood. She was afraid of it all coming back, too, and it would be shortly. "I know, Sam. I'm afraid, too."

"What are you afraid of, Celeste?" The words were a caress, low and soothing.

Could she tell him everything on her mind? She worried about remembering the crash. Had her memory left out a detail that would prove her negligent? "I just want to get there and not think."

"I want to go back to work and not be bombarded with the former me."

The former him? She frowned, keeping her eyes on the road. "You lost me."

"I'm starting to get used to this being my life. The last time I was in my office, I had no clue I would come close to dying. The memories of who I was, what I could do—those are what worry me. I'm not sure about the mental side of going back to work."

That, she got. "It's the same reason why I'm a jittery

mess right now. The mental aspect. Seeing Brandy's church friends, driving past the site. It's scary. I don't blame you for having doubts."

He reached over and put his hand on her shoulder. The touch surprised her, made her want to bend her head and rest her cheek on his hand. "I'm here if you need me for anything. We'll get through it."

We? What a relief to have him to rely on. She sniffed, nodding. He turned the radio to a station playing Christmas music.

"So are you and Parker up for helping me decorate my Christmas tree Saturday afternoon? And by help, I mean you'll basically have to put all the decorations up. Unless I can juggle the crutches somehow."

Celeste laughed. She pictured him smiling, placing candy canes on the tree. "Of course. We'd love to help. I need to decorate my cabin, too, but with Parker walking, I have to be careful."

They discussed her setting up a small tree on a table out of his reach, and before she knew it, she was turning down the road where she and Brandy had spun out. Her breathing quickened, and her palms grew sweaty. She swallowed. Twice.

"This is it, isn't it?" Sam asked. "Do you need to pull over or anything?"

Everything flooded back. Them laughing and singing "A Holly Jolly Christmas." That was the song she'd forgotten. A split second later the wheels had taken a life of their own and the car had spun sideways, sliding, turning. It had hit the ditch with a thud, jerking them around in their seat belts, and the car launched up— they'd both screamed…

And that was when she remembered. She'd reached

for Brandy and held on to her arm the instant before she blacked out.

"Celeste?"

She inhaled and saw the pole. The one her car wrapped around. The one that left her scarred and alone.

It loomed gray and tall and lonely from the field.

You took her from me. You stupid piece of wood.

Her hands clenched the steering wheel as tears began to pour down her cheeks, and a minute later, she drove into the brightly lit church parking lot and cut the engine. Her forehead dropped to her palms, and she shook as she cried.

Sam must have unbuckled because he moved close, putting his arm around her and drawing her to him. She turned, wrapping her arms around his neck.

"I don't understand why, Sam. Why Brandy? Why that night?" *Why not me?*

"Shh…" He brushed her hair from her face. "I don't know. Why don't you tell me about it?"

"We were coming home from shopping. The trunk was full of gifts and wrapping paper. We ate at a Mexican restaurant, and we were having so much fun. Laughing, singing. Brandy had been so tired from the late nights with Parker, and she'd been quiet, depressed since Josh died. She needed a night out. I kept insisting she come with me. And there we were, on our way back to her apartment when the car hit the ice and spun out. The air bags didn't deploy. The officer told my parents it was because of the angle we hit—no sensors were tripped. And I lost her. I lost her."

She let out another cry and held Sam tightly. He rubbed his hand up and down her back, murmuring in the hair against her cheek, "It's okay. It's okay."

When she got her breathing under control, she gazed

into his eyes. She could see it—he wanted to take her pain from her.

The truth had to be told.

"It should have been me." There. She'd said it out loud.

"What?" His eyebrows drew together.

"Why did I get to live and she was taken away? She had a baby, a job as a nurse's aide. The world could have gone on fine without me, but here I am." She wiped the tears from her face with the backs of her hands.

"You're wrong." He stroked her hair. "The world couldn't have gone on fine without you. I don't know why she died, but I know why you lived. The world needs you, Celeste."

She shook her head violently. "Don't say that."

"I will say it." He nudged her chin to look at him. "I'll say it over and over until it gets through that pretty head of yours."

Pretty?

"We should go," she said. "It's almost time for practice."

"Not yet." He shifted closer so their noses were almost touching. "The accident wasn't your fault. Okay?"

Hearing him say those words was like a dose of calming oil on her nerves. The steel keeping her spine rigid dissolved. She knew in her heart it wasn't her fault—it could have happened to anyone—but the aftermath was hard to digest.

"It might not have been my fault, but the results are the same. My best friend is gone, and my nephew—her son—will never know her."

"You told me yourself you're going to make sure Parker knows everything about her."

"It's not the same."

"No, it's not." He took her hand in his. "Being together after this life will have to be enough."

She didn't trust herself to speak. He was right—they'd be together someday. Why wasn't it enough? "I guess I'm selfish. I want her here now." She gave him a halfhearted smile.

"I don't blame you." He ran his hand over his cheek. "I guess I'm selfish, too. I'm glad you're here. I didn't know Brandy, but I'm glad you survived the crash. You've made my life bearable."

She blinked, stunned.

"We'd better go inside." He opened his door, prompting her in motion.

She hurried around the van and got his crutches out of the trunk. When she handed them to him, she covered his hand with hers. "Thanks."

"I meant it. And I mean this—let it go. You can't bring her back."

Maybe she'd been living with too many regrets. She couldn't bring Brandy back. But was it dishonoring her memory to embrace the future?

Sam swung through the church entrance as Celeste held the door open for him. Holding her in his arms moments ago had felt right. More right than he'd felt in a long time. And the fact she'd opened up to him, confided in him, made him feel invincible. Even the fact he was on crutches couldn't dampen his mood.

Did a guy have to be physically whole to consider having a future with a woman? He used to think so, but now he wondered.

"Hello." A frazzled-looking woman appeared in the coat area. She held a clipboard and wore a red-and-white Christmas sweater with kittens on it. She blew a piece of curly brown hair from her eyes. "Are you Celeste?"

"Yes. This is Parker." Celeste took off his stocking

cap. He rubbed his eyes and dropped his head to her shoulder. "Are you Mrs. Roper?"

"No. Sue got the flu. I'm Donna Flack. I understand you're raising Brandy's little boy." She didn't make eye contact with Celeste. Her gaze ran up and down the paper attached to the clipboard. Something about her raised Sam's hackles. "If you'll wait in the fellowship hall with the other parents, we'll get started in a few."

Celeste unzipped Parker's coat. "I'm not sure if he'll do what you need."

"Well, let's hope he can sit on our Mary's lap and act like a baby." She clicked her pen and made a tsk-tsk noise.

"He is a baby." Sam moved next to Celeste. The lady's annoyed tone was rubbing him the wrong way.

"This is Sam Sheffield, Mrs. Flack."

"It's Miss Flack." Her tight smile held no joy. "Well, you know what I mean. If he can sit still, we'll be fine."

Celeste's face fell. "He just started walking, so I'm not sure."

"Shelby Dean is wonderful with babies. She's our Mary, and I have full confidence she'll get him to mind." She pivoted and strode down the hallway to the fellowship hall.

"Get him to mind?" he said. "What did she mean by that?"

"I don't know." She hung up their coats, and they headed in *Miss* Flack's direction. "I'm not sure I want to find out."

"Hey," he said. She stopped and turned to him. "You don't have to do this. It's been a hard night already. We can take off if—"

She shook her head. "No. It's for Grandma Pearl. I'll be okay."

He wasn't so sure, but he had to trust her. They emerged into a large room with groups of parents talking in clusters and kids running around. Laughter and random piano notes filled the air.

"What now?" he whispered. This was out of his element. He'd let Celeste take the lead.

"I have no idea," she whispered back. She set Parker on his feet, but he whirled and held his arms up for her to hold him, which she did.

"May I have your attention?" Miss Flack clapped her hands. "Thank you all for coming. Your children were given their parts in Sunday school last week. I hope they've had a chance to review them. We're going through the recitations tonight and measuring the children for their costumes."

A little girl with braids ran past Miss Flack and chased a towheaded boy.

"Molly, that's enough of that. Both of you stand with your teachers." With a loud sigh, she pointed to a group of kids. "Now, where's Shelby? Matt?"

A pretty dark-haired woman with a wide smile raised her hand. She looked to be in her early twenties. A tall, husky guy joined her. They made a striking couple.

"Everyone meet in the front of the church, and we'll get started." Miss Flack pointed to the doors. "Shelby, Matt, come and meet our baby Jesus."

"I'll be there in a minute," Matt said. "I'm helping Frank get the sets out of the shed."

Sam stood straighter as Shelby and Miss Flack approached, and he sensed Celeste stiffen. He wanted to reassure her, but how? He glanced at her. Sure enough, she'd lowered her face.

She didn't need to do that. She had nothing to be

ashamed of. He hitched his chin, ready to defend or help her. Whatever she needed.

"Shelby, this is Celeste and Parker. She's raising Brandy's little boy."

"We were all sad about what happened." Shelby's brown eyes oozed sincerity. She ran her hand down Parker's back. "It's terrible, this sweet baby losing his mama."

Celeste lifted her face and nodded. Sam ground his teeth together. This Shelby lady seemed nice and all, but did she have any idea how her words were affecting Celeste?

Shelby's eyes widened. "I forgot you were driving."

Sam forced himself to keep his eyes trained on Celeste. He recognized the panic rising, the way her eyes darted. Steadying himself, he placed his hand on her lower back.

"How are you doing?" Shelby continued, her voice comforting. "I'm sure this must have been awful for you."

"Having Parker makes it easier."

"May I?" Shelby smiled and held her hands out.

Celeste nodded, and Shelby took Parker in her arms. "How are you, sweet one?"

Not making a sound, Parker stared into her eyes. He seemed to be studying her. She gave him a little hug and laughed. Sam had to give it to Shelby—she was good with him.

Four young kids ran up to Shelby. "Hi, Miss Shelby. Is that your baby?"

"No, Luke." She grinned at the preschoolers. "This is Parker. He's our baby Jesus this year."

Two girls stared up at Celeste. The one with freckles asked, "What happened to your face?"

Shelby started to reprimand her, but Celeste smiled, shaking her head. "It's fine." She addressed the girl. "I was in a car accident."

"Oh. I'm sorry. It must've hurt pretty bad."

"It did."

Shelby shifted Parker to her hip. "Melissa, do you remember Mrs. Monroe? Brandy? Your aunt Jackie was friends with her."

"The one who died?" The girl's face fell, freckles and all.

Sam wanted to put an end to the conversation. Celeste appeared to be handling it okay, though, so he kept his mouth shut.

"Yes. This is Parker, her baby," Shelby said. "And this is his new mommy."

Celeste cleared her throat and crouched to talk to the kids. "My last name is Monroe, too. Brandy was married to my brother, Josh. She was my best friend in the whole world."

"Is that his daddy?" The blonde girl pointed to Sam.

The question landed in his gut like a brick. If the boat hadn't almost killed him, would he be married by now? With a child of his own?

"He's my neighbor and my friend. Mr. Sheffield."

"Were you in the accident, too?"

Sam belatedly realized the kids expected him to say something.

"No," he said. "I was in a different accident."

"Is your leg broke?" One of the boys eyeballed the crutches.

"Kind of."

"Did it hurt?" Freckles asked.

"Yes. It still does."

"You should get an ice pack." The blonde girl pointed

to him, and he tried not to smile at her serious tone. "My daddy always puts an ice pack on his neck when he gets home from work."

"I'll do that."

The sound of hands clapping interrupted them. "We're waiting for you. Come on, children."

Shelby, still holding Parker, led the way, and the pre-schoolers lined up behind her like they were following the Pied Piper.

"I think Parker is in good hands." Sam waited for Celeste to slip into the back pew and sat beside her, laying his crutches on the floor.

"I do, too."

"You handled that well." He stretched his arm out behind her along the back of the pew.

"You think so?" The tightness in her face disappeared, making her appear younger.

"I know so. You did the right thing letting Parker be in the program." The opening strains of "Joy to the World" blared through the organ. "I want to come with you on Christmas Eve."

She did a double take. "Really? Don't you want to be with your family?"

He loved his family. Always went to church on Christmas Eve with them. But Celeste needed support, and he wanted to give it to her.

"I want to see Parker as baby Jesus. If you don't mind?" He watched her reaction.

She smiled. "I don't mind."

He caught sight of Shelby up there bouncing Parker in her arms and singing.

Before the accident, he hadn't put much thought into having a wife or family. Earlier he'd questioned if he'd

be married now, but he knew better. He'd be opening
his second dealership, married to his job.

Sam clenched his jaw. His job had been fulfilling,
but something had been missing even then. There was
more to life than success. And he wanted more. Could
he have it?

Celeste dropped Sam off at his brother's dealership the
next morning and drove through Lake Endwell. The town
was adorable. Walking around with Sam earlier in the
week had opened her eyes to its charm. Brick storefronts,
pretty awnings, benches on the sidewalks. Everything
was decorated for Christmas. Wreaths hung on doors,
snowflakes were painted on store windows, Christmas
lights were wrapped around trees. Sam had assured her
Bryan would take him home, so she and Parker were
going to explore on their own.

She stopped at City Park. Taking a drink of coffee from
her travel mug, she took in the view of the lake. Last night
had changed her. Sam had changed her. She'd never come
here before because she'd been too self-conscious. She
had even worried about someone staring at her through
her van window.

She shook her head. How foolish. She could see that
now. Their outings had loosened her up, and the success
of being around the kids last night gave her the courage
to break out of the cabin on her own.

Anticipation filled her with energy. The snow from
earlier in the week had melted. It was a great day to
get out.

"What are we waiting for? Let's walk around the
park." She turned to grin at Parker, but her grin slid away
at the sight of his closed eyes. Sleeping. So much for that.

She started the minivan back up. Should she go home?

The blue sky and bluer water in the distance beckoned. No, she wasn't going home. She could sit here and relax awhile. She settled back in the seat and sipped her coffee.

Last night when the little girl had asked her if Sam was Parker's daddy, Celeste hadn't been prepared for her internal reaction. She'd wanted to tell the girl yes, he was his daddy. Spending all this time together, doing the mundane daily stuff, had spoiled her. She relied on Sam. Hadn't understood how lonely she'd been until she moved in next door to him.

What would it be like to come home to a husband? To raise Parker with someone who treated her the way Sam did? To be a family?

She let the glow of possibility wash over her, remembered how strong his arms had felt last night as he'd comforted her. The pressure of his hand against her back when she met Shelby had reassured her. He had the touch. To have those arms around her every day?

She sighed.

She wasn't being realistic. They lived in a bubble. When the real world interrupted—and it would soon— things would change. He'd go back to work. He wouldn't be just hers anymore. It would be good for him to see how important he was again. He'd realize he could have any woman. He'd want a family of his own—not her and her nephew.

She just wished she could stay in the bubble longer.

Sam adjusted his leg in the conference room of Tommy's dealership. A circus had performed in his stomach all morning, and it was all he could do not to stand and pace the room on his crutches. Dad and Bryan hadn't arrived, and Tommy was talking with a customer. What if Sam flipped out the way he had the last time he'd printed out the sales report? If he started crying or had to throw up…

He might as well kiss his career goodbye, because he wouldn't do either in front of the men he respected most. *Get it together, already. If you can't look at a piece of paper without blubbering like a baby, you don't deserve this job.*

He wanted to pray.

I can't pray. I haven't prayed in forever.

God didn't listen, anyhow.

But what if God did? Today?

No, I'm not doing it. I'm not. I can handle this.

"Hey, Sam." Dad charged into the room, jangling his key ring around his finger. "You are a sight for sore eyes, son. I've wanted to see you right there for so long."

Sam's throat tightened. He was going to cry! Right here. Right now.

God, I need Your help. Don't let me fall apart. Not in front of Dad. Don't humiliate me.

He inhaled deeply and began to calm down.

When he trusted himself to speak, Sam said, "I've wanted to be here. It's good to be back."

"You want some coffee?" Dad zoomed straight to the small counter with the coffee supplies.

"Yes." Maybe coffee would scorch his throat free from any inconvenient emotions.

Tommy and Bryan entered the room, laughing about something, and closed the door behind them.

"Look who made it," Tommy teased. "I hope you have a good excuse for missing the last seventy-five meetings."

Sam's stomach did the tango. He wasn't going to throw up, was he? He pressed his hand to his gut.

Bryan winked. "We'll let it slide. As long as you take

over the cost-reduction program. I don't know how you did it, man. It's been driving me crazy."

"I cross-referenced all five dealerships' advertising fees, employee salaries and..." He rattled off the specifics, surprised he remembered the details after all this time. Cost reduction was one of his favorite aspects of the job.

Wait—he didn't feel sick. He didn't want to cry.

"See?" Tommy tapped his temple. "This is why we need you back so bad, Sam. Bryan and I hate that stuff."

Dad slurped his coffee. "I got tired of it, too, boys. The only one who really loved it was my dad. And, apparently, Sam here."

Sam waved two fingers for Bryan to pass him a folder. "Let's see what you've done with this place while I was gone."

As he scanned the first sheet of the report, excitement built.

He wanted to make phone calls and check spreadsheets.

He wanted to joke around with the Sheffield Auto employees again.

Could coming to a meeting really be this easy?

Thank You, God.

This was a gift from the Lord.

Maybe he needed to take his faith one day at a time, too.

Chapter Seven

Sitting in the wheelchair in his bathroom the next afternoon, Sam toweled off his hair and patted aftershave on his neck and face. The loose-fitting jeans weren't his favorite, but they covered his knee brace and allowed him to wear somewhat normal clothes. He'd put on a casual button-down shirt for the occasion. Much better than his usual T and athletic pants. They were decorating the Christmas tree soon.

He wanted today to be special, to repay Celeste for all her kindness. Generosity wasn't his only motive—he enjoyed being with her. He could tell her things he didn't tell other people, including his family. She saw his struggles and didn't seem to think less of him. Lately he'd been thinking about her as more than a friend. And definitely more than the woman next door.

Which brought him to the question: What kind of man did Celeste need?

He was wired to protect and support a woman. If anyone deserved protection and support, it was Celeste. Support he could do once he returned to work. But protect? Might take months or years before he could walk unaided on his own two feet.

The fact he defined himself by his legs was starting to bother him. Could insecurity be a form of pride? *Pride?* In his weak legs? Hardly.

He raked the comb through his hair. The urge to pray pricked at his conscience. For what?

For a future.

What if he started praying regularly? For healing? What if God ignored him again?

Too much was riding on his recovery.

He'd just keep working hard at physical therapy. The harder he worked, the sooner he'd be off these crutches for good. Then he'd be ready for the future he'd been dreaming about. His store numbers were average, which gave him the kick in the pants necessary to build his sales back up, but the company overall was thriving.

If Celeste would drive Sam to their main office twice a week, he could resume his duties as CEO. Or was he getting too ahead of himself? It had been so long that he'd been pumped up about anything. He wanted to rush in and take life by both hands.

He went back to the living room. The artificial tree stood tall and bare in front of the bank of windows. He'd asked Dad to buy it for him. Bryan had set it up this morning. Bryan had also offered to bring Sam's ornaments from his storage unit, but he couldn't remember the combination to the lock, so Bryan ended up poking around in the cottage's basement, unearthing boxes of ornaments, which now sat unopened in the living room. Aunt Sally had dropped an apple pie off earlier.

Surprising himself, he'd told Dad, Bryan and Sally they were welcome to stop by later and see the finished decorations. He wanted to introduce the family to Celeste and Parker. Seeing how well she'd handled being out with strangers the other night, he guessed she was ready for it.

He clip-clopped to the stereo and carefully lowered himself to the ottoman to find a Christmas music station.

Knocks at the door threw his pulse into gear. "Come in."

"Hi. I hope we aren't too early." Celeste shook snowflakes out of her hair and set Parker down. He toddled to Sam as fast as his chubby legs would take him. Once again, Sam regretted not being able to swoop him up and toss him in the air. Parker wrapped his arms around Sam's leg.

"Let's sit down, and I'll hold you." Sam laughed, trying to walk backward with his crutches.

"What smells so good?" Celeste hung her coat over the back of a dining chair.

"Apple pie. Aunt Sally brought it over."

"I see you got the tree up. It's tall, isn't it?" Her hair fell softly over her shoulders. He had to force himself to look away.

"Yeah. Bryan put it up for me." Sam backed to the couch and sat down. Then he picked Parker up and blew raspberries on his tummy. Parker squealed and laughed.

Celeste poked around the boxes. Fat snowflakes meandered down outside. The cinnamon aroma, Christmas music and snow blended together for an enticing effect.

"What should I do first?" Celeste held up a tray of silver bulbs. "Are the lights strung?"

"The tree is pre-lit." He put Parker on the floor and hauled himself up with the crutches. Parker immediately fussed and held his arms in the air for Sam to take him. A pang of regret ricocheted through his heart. He wanted to carry Parker to the tree, put the star in his hands and hoist him up to place it on the tippy-top. But he couldn't. "Sorry, buddy."

Parker plopped on his bottom and started to cry. Sam tried to bend, but his knee felt as though it was going to give way. A flash of heat rippled over his skin. His heartbeat pounded. He forced himself to stay upright and be still a moment. Why couldn't he just bend down and pick the kid up?

"All right, that's enough, Parker." Celeste gave him a stern look, and he sniffled, then crawled to Sam and stared up at him through watery brown eyes. "He'll have to learn you can't carry him around."

The words ripped down his heart. If Sam had kept up with his physical therapy after the last surgery, would his legs be strong enough for a cane?

What did it matter? He couldn't hold Parker *and* use a cane. He needed the balance of both legs.

Parker tugged on Sam's pant legs, tears dripping down his cheeks. Sam clenched his jaw. As much as he didn't want to use his wheelchair in front of Celeste unless absolutely necessary, it would allow him to hold Parker.

Was it worth it?

Whimpering, Parker pulled on Sam's pant leg, and Sam sighed. Yes, Parker was worth it.

"I'll be right back." As soon as he swung the crutches away, Parker began wailing. Sam lowered himself into the chair, balanced the crutches on his lap and wheeled back to the living room. He rolled right to Parker.

"Come on up, buddy."

With watery eyes and a huge grin, Parker stood and held his arms out, and Sam picked him up, settling him on his lap. Parker sighed and snuggled into his chest, sucking his thumb.

Celeste met Sam's eyes, and he forgot to breathe.

Instead of pity in her expression, he saw admiration. Attraction, even.

She was attracted to him? Even in the chair?

Every muscle fiber ached to stand up, to drag her in his arms, to run his fingers through her silky brown hair, to press his lips against hers. To kiss her.

But Parker's warm body had melded into his side, and Sam could no more pluck the child from his lap than he could act on his fantasies. So he wheeled to the nearest box and, with his free hand, grabbed a sealed plastic bag full of ornaments.

"Let's get this decorated." He sounded like a drill sergeant, but what else could he do? *God, I know I'm out of line here. It's been a long time since I've prayed on a regular basis, but I don't know how to handle this—how to handle these feelings for Celeste. Will You help me?*

Celeste was hanging bulbs around the tree. She moved near Sam and stretched to place one close to the top. Her slender waist was right there in front of him. Within reach. The urge to hold her grew stronger.

Great. That's not helping.

Parker's little body radiated heat through Sam's shirt, and soon his even breathing assured Sam he'd fallen asleep. He better get his mind off Celeste and onto the task at hand. He ripped the bag open and pulled out a Mrs. Claus felt ornament.

Who had spent money on this thing?

"This is the ugliest ornament I've ever seen." He gave it a skeptical stare. "It looks like a cat toy."

She tipped her head to the side to see it. Her sparkly eyes did something to his pulse. "It's not so bad."

"How can you say that? This gal looks like she hasn't seen daylight since 1954." He drew out a matching Santa. "It gets worse. They're a pair."

Celeste laughed, loud and tinkling. "Well, be thankful there aren't matching reindeer."

"Wrong." Sam held the clear bag up. Several brown felt reindeer with gold cording winding around them were visible.

"Oh, my." She tucked her lips under in an attempt not to laugh. "Aren't these your decorations?"

"No. They're Granddad's."

Celeste smiled and lifted her knuckle under her chin. "When do you think they were last on a tree?"

"Like I said, 1954." He blew dust off a small brown box.

"How sweet. Think of all the memories here. I wonder if your grandparents bought or made them. Maybe they were gifts. I can imagine a young couple, newly married, decorating a tree with all of these. Can you?"

"I do remember an old picture. Grandma had a blond beehive, and Granddad's hair was slicked back. He had his arm slung around her, and they both were laughing."

"I'd love to see it." Celeste dug through a paper bag. "Where did they live?"

He thought back to what he knew of his grandparents. "They built a small brick ranch in town when they were first married. A few years later, after Granddad made his first dealership profitable, they built a larger house in the country."

Celeste held up a painted glass ornament shaped like a cone. "Were they happy?"

"Yeah. They were. They built this cabin before I was born. Grandma died when I was young, though, so I don't remember much about her. But Granddad was great. Lived here as long as I can remember."

"These boxes are like a time capsule. I wish your grandparents were still around so we could ask them

about their first Christmases." She carefully threaded
a hook through a pink felt ballerina. "Sam?"

"Hmm?" He untangled the reindeer. Something in her
posture made him think she had more than his grandparents on her mind.

"What do you want your memories to look like?"

He stretched Rudolph apart from Dancer and Prancer.
"I'm not sure. Everything kind of got divided pre and
post accident for me. Before? I planned on getting my
dealership to the point it was consistently making enough
money so I could build another one in the next county.
My life revolved around my ambition. I really wasn't
looking for anything else."

"But now?" she asked quietly as she placed the ballerina next to a ceramic kitten on the tree.

He glanced at Parker snuggled into his side, then met
Celeste's rich eyes, full of expectation. How honest should
he be?

"More has been on my mind. Family."

She blinked, a smile lighting up her face.

Sam patted Parker's head and untangled the final reindeer. "When I'm out of this chair and off these crutches,
I'll put more thought into it. I do know this guy has me
wrapped around his pinkie."

"Did you hear something from your doctor?"

"No, but I'm counting on it." He was no longer willing to accept a lifelong disability. He'd made consider-
able strides over the last month. But what if something
happened? Another accident? Another slip? "I'll figure
the rest out when I'm on both feet again."

Furrows dipped in her forehead and the light in her
eyes faded.

"What about you?" he asked.

She selected beaded candy canes and disappeared behind the tree. "Today will be a good memory."

Why did he have the feeling he'd just let her down?

An hour later the Christmas tree was crammed with a combination of painted glass ornaments and a huge assortment of felt reindeer as well as Mr. and Mrs. Claus—or the Ugly Couple, as Sam called them. Celeste admired the view before slipping into the kitchen to start the coffeemaker. The white lights cast a charming glow, their reflections bouncing off the windows. She didn't want today to end. She enjoyed existing in this snow globe where Sam looked at her as if she was special. How long would it last?

They'd set Parker, still sleeping, on a folded blanket on the fluffy area rug in the living room. He'd be able to finish his nap safely there. The late afternoon sky was growing darker, and the snow that had fallen all day coated the ground by at least an inch. She peeked out the kitchen window. Maybe two inches. She hoped so.

From the minute Sam rolled into the living room in the wheelchair to accommodate Parker, Celeste had been losing the battle warring in her heart. She was getting too attached to Sam. Dare she admit, even to herself, she was halfway in love with him? And the flirty mood earlier hadn't helped—not one bit. How could she protect herself from getting hurt when Sam stared at her *that* way? Or when he casually mentioned he'd been thinking of families?

Did he have any idea how many times she'd caught herself wishing they were a family? That Parker had him as a dad and that she had Sam as a husband?

But then he'd iced the atmosphere with his comment about walking on two feet before thinking about having more. She'd watched enough of Sam's physical therapy sessions since she'd met him to know he had no guarantees he'd walk unassisted again.

Would he let his physical limitations decide his future?

Like she was one to talk. Her mirror revealed the truth every time she glanced its way. Her life was on hold for the same reasons.

Maybe they were both being selfish.

Nonsense.

Falling in love with him was all wrong, and she was the one who would lose. She knew he was terrific, and it was only a few weeks before he'd be back out and about in Lake Endwell every day. He'd see other women, reminding him he had options. Ones that didn't include a scarred single mom.

Christmas music still played in the background, and the apple pie beckoned. She rummaged through drawers until she found a knife and serving utensils.

"Ready for a break?" She held up the pie as Sam approached on his crutches.

"Definitely. Is that coffee I smell?" His blue eyes twinkled with something she couldn't decipher, but whatever it was, it overrode her admonitions to keep her feelings in check. He stopped close to her. Closer than usual. He smelled fantastic, all spicy and manly and...

"Coffee. Yes." She took a tiny step back, but Sam leaned toward her.

"I'd offer to carry it but..."

Was he teasing? She searched his face. He sure was. She forced a lighthearted laugh. "Oh, no. Your hands are full, and we don't want to lose this pie."

"True." He nodded, faking concern with an insincere frown. "Aunt Sally's pie should never be wasted."

"Exactly." She could feel the warmth of his body near hers. He seemed taller. But that might be because she wasn't usually inches away from him. She had to tilt her chin up to meet his eyes. Which was probably a mistake, considering her mouth dried like tissue paper as soon as she did. Those cheekbones. That face. His bottom lip was fuller than the top lip. But why was she thinking about that?

And the way he looked at her? Made her think he had feelings for her, too.

Shrugging slightly, she sidestepped around him and carried the dessert in her jittery hands to the table. Then she returned to the kitchen for plates and silverware. Her fingers trembled as she opened cupboards. Finally, she wiped her hands down her jeans. "Do you want a slice of pie now or do you want to wait until the coffee is ready?"

"Let's wait. Come here a minute." He swung the crutches to the living room, and she followed. He took a seat on the couch and patted the spot next to him. She raised her eyebrows, her skin tingling—what was he up to?—and sat down, hands folded primly in her lap.

Taking something off the end table, he turned and faced her. "Look what I found."

Oh, my.

He lifted his hand above her head, and she looked up. Mistletoe.

Mistletoe? Her heartbeat was tripping over itself.

"You know the tradition, right?" he asked, huskily.

She had no words. Just a million and one impressions. Her mouth opened before she had time to think. "It represented peace to the Romans, protection from death to the Nordic people, and in Victorian England, it was a big deal if a girl refused a kiss. She wouldn't find a suitor the next year."

His face blanked, and then he grinned. "Well, I have my own rules about it."

"What rules?"

"The mistletoe rules." He leaned in, smiling, his blue eyes intent. His right hand caressed her hair before settling behind her neck. He drew her closer to him. Firm hands, the smell of his skin, warm breath all collided as his lips brushed hers.

Before she could process the sensation, his lips pressed more insistently, but not demanding. She relaxed into his arms and followed his lead. Her arms wound round his neck, and she reveled in the softness of the hair at his nape. Kissing him felt so right, even better than her dreams. If they could freeze this moment—she could live right here, right now, forever.

Sam's kiss tapered off, and he searched her eyes, his lips spreading into a satisfied smile. Their faces were almost touching. The slightest movement and he'd be kissing her again.

"What were the rules?" she whispered.

"Rule number one. I've wanted to—"

"Yoo-hoo!" The door opened and a gust of snowy air blew in, bringing with it a noisy group of people led by a short blonde older lady wearing fake reindeer antlers on her head.

Sam rolled his eyes, muttering, "Perfect timing."

She squinted. Was Claire behind the antler lady?

Let the earth swallow her now.

Celeste kept her spine as straight as the flagpole in front of the cottage. Laughter and conversation spilled inside with the rest of the crowd. Two of the tall men were clearly Sam's brothers, but the other two? She had no idea. As the adults shrugged out of their coats, a little dark-haired girl, six or seven, ran straight to Sam and fell into his arms.

"Uncle Sam, I got you something." The beautiful child kissed his nose. "Want to see?"

"Of course I do, Macy."

She ran back to the kitchen, disappearing in a sea of legs.

"Sam," Claire yelled, her face glowing. "Where did you find Granddad's old ornaments? These bring me back." With her hand on her tiny belly, she shook her head in wonder and stepped back to survey the tree.

Celeste swallowed her mortification and stood. She hadn't talked to Claire since moving next door. She needed to congratulate her.

"And what a great surprise to see you here, Celeste." Claire rushed forward, taking Celeste's hands in hers. Claire kissed her on the cheek, and Celeste was so surprised she couldn't find a single word to say. "Did Sam rope you into decorating for him? I hope he hasn't been a slave driver with this tree."

"Congratulations. I hear you're expecting." Celeste nodded to Claire's tummy.

"Thank you," she said, her eyes growing damp. "We had a hard time getting pregnant."

A commotion made them both turn.

"Hey, watch the baby." Sam glared at two of the men and wielded his right crutch to point at Parker. "And for crying out loud, don't wake him up." His eyes met Celeste's, and he tilted his head to the side. "Come on, I'll introduce you to everyone."

"Let me move Parker first."

The next fifteen minutes were spent meeting an

endless supply of Sheffield siblings, wives, husbands, nieces, his aunt Sally and uncle Joe and, finally, his dad.

"Glad to meet you," Dale Sheffield said. He wasn't as tall as his sons, but he seemed energetic. He had a thick head of silver hair and the kindest blue eyes she'd ever seen. "I see you got the tree decorated. Reminds me when I was a kid. I didn't know the old man saved all those decorations."

Aunt Sally scampered over, antlers jiggling. "Look, Dale, I haven't seen those reindeer in years. Remember how Ma made us put them up every Christmas?"

"They were ugly then, and they're ugly now." Dale crossed his arms over his chest. "But she sure loved them."

"Well, you know why, don't you?" Sally shifted her weight to the side, putting a hand on her hip. "She and Dad didn't have any money those first two years they were married."

"I know, I know."

Sally glared at him, then turned to Celeste. "Our mother hated the idea of a bare tree, so she and her sister made all these ornaments out of felt. Hours of cutting, embroidering, sewing and stuffing. She was so proud of them she put them up every year, even when they had enough money to decorate with crystal."

Dale chuckled. "Dad said the same thing each time they lugged them out. 'If it wasn't for your mother's resourcefulness, Sheffield Auto never would have survived the first years.' I think he might have been prouder of those homemade decorations than she was."

Sally nodded, a soft gleam in her eyes. "Yeah, they appreciated each other, that's for sure."

A couple approached. Celeste tried to remember the man's name. Tom? He looked like an older, darker, more mischievous version of Sam. "It was good to have you back yesterday."

Sam grinned. "It was good to be back."

Tom pointed at Sam. "Now you have no excuse. Macy's singing in church with her Sunday school class Wednesday night. It would make us happy if you came and watched her."

"Why Wednesday?"

"Did you forget about that thing called Advent?"

"Oh, right."

Parker's cry alerted Celeste he'd finally woken. She excused herself and picked him up. His cheeks were flushed from sleep, and he rubbed his eyes with one fist and clung to her neck with the other.

She took him to the spare bedroom and changed his diaper. When she returned, cheerful chatter filled the room, and one of the women approached. Tom's wife, Stephanie? Sam had introduced them only minutes ago—she hoped she got the name right.

"Your little boy is so cute." She held a toddler girl with dark brown curls. "I know we can be overwhelming. I'm Stephanie, and this is Emily. How old is he?"

Celeste caught a glimpse of the other men. The dark blond who seemed quieter than the others was Bryan. The other two men were Claire's and Libby's husbands, Reed and Jake, and they happened to be brothers.

"Parker turned a year in October. What about Emily?"

"She'll be eighteen months in a few weeks." The girl wriggled for Stephanie to put her down. As soon as her feet hit the floor, she took off running to Claire. Stephanie shook her head, grinning. "She is a handful. Everyone calls her Sweetpea, but trust me, she's less sweet and more tart."

Celeste laughed. "Yeah, Parker's been starting to

cry more when he doesn't get his way. He's kind of obsessed with Sam."

"Well, Sam's good with kids."

A petite, stylish woman with green eyes materialized next to them.

"How are the Christmas products selling, Jade?" Stephanie asked. She shook her head, addressing Celeste. "Where are my manners? Have you two met? Celeste, this is Jade, Bryan's wife."

Jade grinned, her eyes sparkling brighter than the lights on the tree. "We were introduced a little bit ago, but I'm terrible with names, so if you ever forget mine, I won't be offended."

Celeste smiled, and Jade turned to Stephanie. "Libby and I ordered handmade ornaments. Metal, wood, glass. They are gorgeous. You should stop by and check them out. Bring the girls."

"Did I hear my name?" A stunning blonde, the youngest of Sam's siblings, approached Stephanie and Jade, putting an arm around each of their shoulders.

"I was just telling Stephanie and Celeste about the ornaments." Jade practically wiggled in excitement. "Celeste, have you met Libby?"

Celeste nodded, fascinated by the interaction.

"We're so thankful for you," Libby said. She glanced over her shoulder at the men. "Sam's himself again. Because of you."

"I didn't really…" Celeste wasn't sure what to say.

"Yes, you did, but I'll drop it for now." Libby winked. "So, I went to the Ann Arbor art fair this summer and met the most amazing artists…"

"Do you two work together?" Celeste asked when Libby finished telling them about the hand-stamped metal ornaments.

"Yes! Jade opened a T-shirt shop almost two years ago, wasn't it?" Libby asked. Jade nodded, so she continued. "After she married Bryan—thank you a million times over for making him happy—we decided to join forces and expand the store. Shine Gifts is now double the size. You might have seen it downtown Lake Endwell. We have a purple—"

"Eggplant," Jade interjected.

"Excuse me, eggplant—" Libby grinned, scrunching her nose "—awning over the front door. Stop in anytime."

"I design and make the custom shirts and bags and such." Jade waved her hands as if to say "ta-da."

"And I find the jewelry, books, art and gifts." Libby drew Jade in for a one-armed hug. "We make a great team."

"I heard you run your own virtual assistant business, Celeste," Stephanie said. "I know at least four businesses who would jump at the chance to hire you part-time."

"Really?" Celeste let the possibility wash over her. More work meant more money, which she needed, but she already had a hard time fitting in the clients she had. She wouldn't need to hustle for more work if she went through with her teacher certification. She could raise Parker on a modest teacher's wage. Until then, though, she'd have to consider new business contacts. "Feel free to give them my number. I'll leave a business card with Sam next time I come over." Parker started getting antsy in her arms, so she set him down, keeping an eye on him as he headed toward Macy. The little girl crouched as he approached and ruffled his hair as she smiled.

"Macy loves babies," Stephanie said as Macy took Parker's hand. "You might never get him back."

"She's darling." Celeste watched Macy slowly walk with Parker to the tree. She pointed out ornaments, and he stared at her, mesmerized. Sam chatted with his brothers and uncle a few feet from the tree.

Celeste met Sam's eyes across the room. They shimmered with appreciation. Heat flashed up her neck, and instantly, she thought of their kiss. The pressure of his lips against hers. The strength and tenderness of his hands. The feeling of being cherished.

As much as she enjoyed the interaction with his family, she wouldn't mind if they all disappeared, leaving her and Sam alone. To have him explain the mistletoe rules a little more in depth.

But she shook the ungracious thought away. His family was wonderful. None of them had asked about her face. They all treated her as if she didn't have scars. For a few moments, she'd forgotten about them.

A burst of laughter filled the air from the men. She closed her eyes, savoring this—a house full of fun people on a winter day surrounded by Christmas scents, twinkly lights and laughter.

If things were different…

But they weren't. Maybe she and Sam were both indulging in wishful thinking. She kept pretending life would change with more surgery, and he pretended his legs would somehow spontaneously heal.

She'd have to hold on to the memory of today forever, because her gut told her the snow globe they were in was about to shatter.

Chapter Eight

"What am I going to do with all this?" Sam leaned against the kitchen counter and shook his head in amazement at the plastic containers full of sugar cookies, bowls of frosting in pastel colors and every type of sprinkle imaginable. He and Celeste had just returned from his Monday therapy session. For two days he hadn't stopped thinking about their kiss. In fact, he couldn't get Celeste off his mind. And he needed to. Soon.

"Um, wow." Celeste crossed her arms over her chest and bit her lower lip, but her eyes danced with laughter. Parker played with a toy car on the floor.

"Aunt Sally's finally lost it."

"Did she mention anything about this to you?"

"Nope. No, she did not." He lifted his eyes to the ceiling. "Aunt Sally texted me she was dropping something off, but what was she thinking? There's enough sugar here to give someone diabetes."

"Is that a note?" Celeste pointed to a sheet of paper wedged under a package of plastic pastry bags. He scanned the note.

I made too many cookies and thought that darling baby might enjoy decorating them with his pretty mama and you. Love, Aunt Sally.

Uneasiness prickled over his skin. As much as he wanted to spend the day decorating cookies with Celeste and Parker, he knew it wasn't wise. He had to stop thinking about himself and start thinking about what was best for her. Which wasn't him.

She plucked the paper from his hand. "Isn't that sweet? Thinking of Parker."

Thinking of setting him up with Celeste was more like it. His aunt had a history of matchmaking. Didn't his aunt realize Celeste was special? That she needed a guy who could be there for her in ways he couldn't? Her slender arms carried too much every day as it was. He would not be another burden on her.

"Why don't you change, and I'll get everything ready?" Her clear brown eyes held no questions or concerns. Just anticipation.

What was he supposed to do now? Tell her to hit the road? That she couldn't stay because his heart was getting in way too deep? Yeah, that would go over well.

"Okay."

When he'd changed, he paused a moment in the doorway. Celeste had laid the cookies out on wax paper at the dining table. Parker was strapped into his portable booster seat. He nibbled on one cookie and banged another against the table. She was spooning the icing into the pastry bags. The Christmas tree twinkled beside them.

What had been an empty cottage had become a warm, inviting home.

What would it hurt if he simply enjoyed being with them today?

He took a seat next to Parker and pretended to take a bite from his cookie. Parker squealed, snatching the cookie back. Then he thrust it back to Sam, and Sam laughed, pretending to take another bite. The boy laughed harder. Sam made gobbling noises, egging him on.

Celeste set the bags of frosting on the table, and he almost caught his breath. She looked happy. Beautiful.

He cleared his throat. "What do you do with this?" Picking up a squishy bag full of baby blue frosting, he tried to shake his head of all the warm fuzzy feelings invading him.

Her fingers brushed his as she demonstrated how to pipe the icing onto the cookie. "Easy, huh?"

"Yeah." It was. Easy. All of this was too easy.

And it wouldn't last.

He knew better than to count on it. It was one thing to be friends, another to kiss her, and still another to fall in love. He'd never been in love before. He'd liked casual dating, enjoyed dinner and a movie. This…this doing regular everyday stuff with Celeste and Parker compelled him. He'd rather hang out and decorate cookies with them than anything else. But it wasn't fair to her.

Parker stared up at him through big hopeful eyes, the cookie stretched toward Sam's mouth. Once more he pretended to gobble the cookie.

"Are you going to help or do I have to crack the whip?" Celeste popped her hand on her hip in mock anger.

"Okay, I'll get at it, boss." He frosted a snowman cookie and sifted colored sugar on top. Celeste sat across from him, and she carefully decorated the cutout cookies. After a while, Parker got antsy, so she took him out of the high chair and let him play with his car again.

Contentment crept up on him. He watched Celeste's lips curve into a slight smile as she put the finishing touches on a cookie shaped like a snowflake. Simple pleasures. Ones he craved. The only way he could justify spending all this time together was if he knew for sure he'd be walking on his own soon.

Maybe it was time to ask Dr. Stepmeyer about his progress. How long would it be before he could have a real life?

Another Wednesday at physical therapy, another round of torture.

With his right leg, Sam lifted the exercise table's torque arm, straining to get it high enough. His thigh muscles protested, but not as much as his stiff knee. Sweat dripped down both sides of his forehead. At least his hour was almost up.

He ground out the remaining sets and slumped, reaching for the towel and water he kept nearby. After a long drink, he sucked in another breath and willed his legs to stop twitching and shooting fire.

Dr. Stepmeyer returned. He stretched his neck from side to side. "Can I ask you something?"

"Of course."

"Do you think it's working?"

"Yes. Don't you? I thought your progress was obvious." She handed him his crutches and strolled to the treatment table. When he was ready, she hooked up the electrodes and started the machine.

"You came in here five weeks ago in a wheelchair. You could barely stand on your left leg and couldn't put any weight on your right. Your left leg is strong now. Much stronger than it was. The right knee still can't take much pressure, but yes, your time and effort are paying off."

"I need to go back to work."

"I figured." She sat on the stool next to him, her clipboard in her lap. "Have you looked at your leg lately, Sam?"

He glanced down. Purple scars spiraled around it, and parts of his thigh and knee appeared to have been carved out, chunks missing. "Yeah. What about it?"

"We see the outside, but we don't know what's going on inside. When is your next doctor appointment?"

His leg may be ugly, but it was whole. He'd purposely tried not to think about what was going on inside it. The nerve was supposed to reconnect. That was the whole point of the nerve graft. "Dr. Curtis warned me healing would be slow."

"He was right," she said, nodding. "But these surgeries don't always restore full function. Dr. Curtis warned you about that, too."

"What are you saying?" he snapped. The odors of the room assaulted him—sweat, sweat and more sweat.

"I'm saying, keep working hard. Make an appointment with him before you go back to work."

"I'm going back in January."

"Okay. But be careful. And protect your leg as much as possible." She set the clipboard down and swiped her tablet. Clicking her tongue, she read whatever was on the screen. "During our initial interview, you told me you spent seventy-five percent of the workday on your feet before the accident. Will you modify that?"

He sighed. "I'll try."

"You're going to have to do more than try, Sam. Don't expect work to be the same."

"Nothing is the same, is it?" He grabbed the water

bottle and took another drink. If only she'd hook the electrodes up to his flaming emotions. Release the tension every word she said brought on. "I'm going to be using a cane soon. I have to."

"You're not ready." Her mouth twisted in disapproval.

"I am ready. Ready to move on with my life. The crutches are impossible. I can't use my hands for anything, and I'm tired of having to wear a man-purse to carry something from one room to another. How can I shake a customer's hand if I'm worried my crutches will fall?"

"That's why you need to talk to Dr. Curtis before returning to work."

"So what are you saying? If he doesn't clear me, I'm stuck at home?"

"I don't know. That's your call. You might be better off using the wheelchair at work. You can keep coming here three times a week and use the crutches at home."

"I'm not going to work in a wheelchair." He stared at the wall. All this work and for what? Nothing?

"Hey, normally I'd agree with you. I want you out of the wheelchair as much as possible. But I don't want you collapsing on the floor with a muscle strain. Or worse. Think about it."

Dr. Stepmeyer shut off the machine, carefully detached the electrodes and told him to go down the hall.

If this place had a punching bag, he was ready to go nine rounds with it. Instead, he made his way to the hall. All the prayers he'd pleaded last year roared back. How many times had he begged to be blessed with the ability to walk on his own?

The urge to ask again hit him hard, but he shook it away.

He didn't care that God ignored him or that Dr. Stepmeyer thought he should wait. He was tired of waiting for his life to turn around.

He'd go back to work. He'd stay on his crutches. Soon, he'd walk with a cane.

He'd show them all.

"How did it go?" Celeste drove out of the physical rehab center's parking lot after Sam buckled himself in. They'd decided to make their first appearance at Lake Endwell Library today to pick up Christmas picture books for Parker. It had been over a year since Celeste had been in a library or bookstore, and she couldn't wait.

"It went fine." Sam kept his head turned away, staring out his window. The way he said it told her it was not fine.

"Did something happen?" She turned left at the stoplight on their way out of the city. The air had a bite to it, and the snow from the weekend still covered the ground. Had it been only four days since he'd kissed her? She'd mentally relived it about four hundred times since then, but who was counting? He'd been so wonderful with Parker when they'd decorated the cookies, but she'd been a wee bit disappointed that he'd kept his distance from her. He certainly hadn't attempted to kiss her again.

"No," he barked. "Let's drop it."

She sat up straighter. *Well, then.*

Tempted to ask, to push him for details, she gritted her teeth and cranked the country music louder.

He flicked the radio off.

"What is wrong with you?" She didn't even try to keep the exasperation out of her tone.

"Nothing."

"Do you still want to go to the library?" *Please say yes.*

"Why wouldn't I?" He crossed his arms over his chest, not looking at her.

"You tell me."

He didn't respond.

Wonderful.

She'd gone into full-blown dreamy schoolgirl mode, unable to contain her enthusiasm about seeing Sam again. And Sam? Seemed as enthusiastic as an angry raccoon.

But why?

The miles sped by without conversation. Bare trees and evergreens lined the side of the road. As they neared Lake Endwell, her irritation mounted.

She hated the silent treatment. Didn't she have enough to worry about right now? Like the upcoming evaluation by her plastic surgeon? And what about her home life? She was regularly staying up past midnight to meet her clients' needs and was so tired in the afternoon she'd taken to napping with Parker. She'd gotten an email this morning from her top client. They wanted to double her hours after the holidays. How was she going to keep up?

With one hand on the steering wheel, she rubbed her left temple. The work didn't fulfill her. Sure, she was organized and good at her job, but she found it boring. She wanted to share her love of history with others as a teacher. If she was this busy trying to raise Parker and make ends meet, how would she find time to take the online courses she needed to get certified?

Lake Endwell Library came into view. She found a spot, and minutes later, with Parker in her arms, she held the door open for Sam and followed him inside.

It smelled like books. She closed her eyes and smiled. Books—the best smell in the world.

"Mama! Mama!" Parker bounced in her arms. She set him down, keeping a firm hold on his hand.

"Stay with me, Parker. Let's go find the children's section." She didn't bother looking Sam's way as she led Parker to the corner with hot-air balloons painted on the walls. Miniature hot-air balloons in assorted primary colors hung from the ceiling, too. Very cute.

Parker toddled to a table with wooden puzzles. Celeste helped him sit in a tiny chair. She browsed the picture books while he played. An adorable Christmas book with a big brown bear on the cover caught her eye. She flipped through, smiling at the beautiful illustrations. How did artists do it? Create such imaginative pages conveying different moods?

Within minutes she'd collected a pile of picture books. Parker was still happily clanging the big wooden puzzle pieces against the forms. Someone had left a stack of magazines and books on the table, so she sat in one of the tiny chairs and eyed the titles.

A celebrity magazine, a Southern cookbook, two mystery novels and a nonfiction book. The nonfiction piqued her interest. Something about being okay after life falling apart.

She itched to pick it up and read the back cover, but what if the person who'd selected it came back? Would they think she was poaching their book?

With a turn of her head to the left then the right, she tried to locate who might be checking out this pile. A librarian stood behind a counter. An older man near the fireplace read a newspaper with one ankle on his knee. Sam stood in front of the shelves with the DVDs. Her gaze lingered on his broad shoulders.

What had put him in such a bad mood? She nibbled her fingernail. Was it something she'd said?

She snatched the book. It was written from a Christian viewpoint. She sighed. It probably was going to drone on about how life will be perfect if you just trust in God enough.

Life wasn't perfect. No matter how much she trusted God.

After flipping it over, she read the opening line of the back cover. *Life isn't perfect for Christians or anyone.*

Huh. Maybe she should give this one a try.

The bullet points reiterated the theme: *God will help you survive any circumstances.* It promised the secrets of having peace regardless of your trials and recognizing how something good can come from something bad.

She needed this book.

Opening to the first chapter, she began reading. And she didn't look up until Sam stood next to her. She sensed his presence before he cleared his throat. "Are you ready?"

"Sure." She rose, checking on Parker. He still sat at the table, but now he was flipping the pages of a board book with a caterpillar on the cover. "Did you get what you wanted?"

"Yeah." His posture wasn't as stiff as earlier.

"Would you watch him for me while I check out?" Celeste hauled the picture books into her arms, and she set the nonfiction back on the other pile.

"Of course."

She walked in the direction of the front desk, but on a whim, she turned to the computer. Maybe the library had more than one copy of the book she'd left on the table. If not, she could put a hold on it. She typed in a search of the title, and when she saw they had another one available, she almost raised her hand for a fist pump. It took only a minute to find the book.

At the checkout desk, the librarian blinked when

she registered her scars, but Celeste just smiled. Books made everything better. She didn't have the energy to be self-conscious, not when she couldn't wait to carve out a few hours to read.

She wanted to find out how God could make something good come out of something so bad. Was it even possible?

"I'm all set." She approached Sam and Parker. With one hand full of books, she attempted to pick Parker up. She almost lost her balance, but on the second try, she settled him on her hip. Kissed his soft cheek. "You ready to go home?"

He wrapped his arms around her neck.

They left the warmth of the library for the cold wind outdoors. Strange, but having the book in her possession made her not care if Sam was grumpy or mad at her. She didn't want to analyze his mood.

"Do you need anything else?" She started the van. "Want me to stop anywhere?"

"No. I'm ready to go home."

Disappointed, she nodded. He didn't want to be with her. *Good.* She had a book to read. Work to do. Her life to figure out.

The problem? It was all easier with Sam by her side.

Even if she shoved her romantic feelings underground, she couldn't imagine forging forward with her new life if Sam wasn't a part of it.

She glanced at his profile. Serious. Reflective.

Unfortunately, she had no guarantees their friendship would last.

Chapter Nine

Sam followed Bryan and Jade into the pew later that night. He hadn't been to church in a year and a half. Was he ready to trust God again? He wasn't sure, but if not, why was he here?

For Macy. And Tom and Stephanie. He loved his niece, and it was time to support her the way his family had been supporting him. And he felt guilty about being short with Celeste earlier, but there was only so much bad news he could take.

Soft strains of "Angels We Have Heard on High" filled the room along with the smell of freshly lit candles. The stained glass windows appeared dark, the scenes difficult to see at night. Kind of like his mental state. Difficult to discern. Sam opened the program. Five hymns. From the looks of it, the service would be long. He stretched his leg out.

The pastor welcomed everyone, and the opening hymn played on the organ. He shouldn't have taken his annoyance out on Celeste. She understood him without judging him. He liked their small talk, the ease of being with her.

It would be simple to have that ease back, but how could he lead Celeste on?

If he went to the doctor and found out he wasn't cleared for work, he didn't know what he'd do. The facts were there—out of work, couldn't drive, couldn't walk—basically helpless. What woman wanted that combination in a man?

Maybe he hadn't been leading her on. Maybe the doctor would clear him for work.

The pastor motioned for everyone to rise. Sam gripped the back of the pew in front of him and hauled himself to his feet, careful not to put too much weight on his right leg. He joined in a responsive reading and soon was sitting again.

Sam relaxed as the pastor read the sermon text, then preached about Jesus's birth from Mary's perspective.

"Picture a young woman, thrust into a drama she hadn't expected. First, she's visited by an angel and finds out she's going to be the mother of the promised Savior. Then she almost loses her fiancé because of the baby, and instead of enjoying the pregnancy in familiar surroundings, she's forced on a long, strenuous trip to Bethlehem, where she gives birth in lowly circumstances."

Sam folded his hands in his lap. He hadn't put much thought into Mary at Christmas.

The pastor continued, "And what about Joseph? Here's a man who was shocked to find out his bride-to-be was carrying a child. A visit from an angel explained the baby was from the Holy Spirit, but I'm guessing it was a lot to take in. On top of that, they're forced to travel to Bethlehem at a time Joseph would most want to protect Mary. The town was so crowded. Joseph couldn't even provide proper lodging for them. They had to use a manger for a crib. Most husbands don't want their pregnant wives making a difficult journey, and they certainly don't want their baby to sleep in a feeding trough."

Joseph's issues? Sam understood. Of course Joseph wanted to protect Mary. If it was Sam, he would have knocked on every innkeeper's door and demanded a room, which, now that he thought about it, Joseph probably did.

Why hadn't God given them a room? He'd sent angels to Mary and Joseph, explaining what was happening, but He wouldn't give them a comfortable bed?

"Sometimes God's ways don't fit in with our expectations," the pastor said. "We expect God's Son to be born in luxury, not his humble beginnings in the small town of Bethlehem. All-powerful but with no earthly kingdom. It's almost incomprehensible God would send His beloved Son to earth to die for our sins."

Sam frowned. If he had a son, he'd protect him and not let anything bad happen to him.

"But Jesus didn't stay dead. He conquered death. This Christmas season I hope you focus on this—God loves you so much He sent His son to live a perfect life, to die for you, and to rise again so that you can have eternal life. This is the real Christmas gift. The gift of salvation by grace alone."

"Amen," the congregation said.

Piano chords filled the church, and Sam shifted to watch two rows of children march up the aisle. Macy's ringlets bounced above her dark purple dress. When they were lined up, they began to sing "O Little Town of Bethlehem."

He bowed his head, surprised at the emotion pressing against his chest. Jesus never had it easy. Born poor. Tempted by the devil. His friends betrayed Him. And He was crucified even though He'd never done a wrong thing.

Sam swallowed to loosen his tight throat. Jesus's entire life had been filled with struggles—and He not only *was* God but was loved by God. Jesus could have led an easy life. He could have hopped right off the cross, but He refused.

Maybe Sam had been wrong all this time.

Maybe God did care about him.

Could God have plans for him that he didn't understand? He glanced sideways at Bryan, who had his arm draped over Jade's shoulders. Sam hoped so.

He wanted a family of his own. Mary and Joseph had made it work, and they had a lot of obstacles to overcome.

He needed to apologize to Celeste. Make an effort with her. Be the friend to her that she'd been to him. Their friendship was growing into more, and maybe he didn't need to fight it. Maybe it was time to do something together just the two of them.

After the service ended, he gathered with the rest of his family in the large entryway.

"Nice singing up there, Sunshine." Sam winked at Macy.

"Thanks for coming, Uncle Sam." She hugged him. Her pretty blue eyes sparkled. "Are you coming over for cocoa?"

"Umm…"

"Are you up for it?" Bryan asked him as he helped Jade into her coat. "We'll drive you."

"I think I am." Sam nodded as Macy jumped up and down, clapping.

"I'm going to tell Mommy!" She ran to where Tom and Stephanie chatted with a few other parents.

So simple to make Macy happy. Showing up really

wasn't hard. Why had he convinced himself it was? Asking Celeste on a date might not be hard, either.

"How do you two feel about kids?" Sam asked Bryan and Jade.

A look of terror crossed Bryan's face, but Jade grinned. "We love kids, don't we, Bryan?"

His brother visibly gulped.

"I'm going to ask Celeste out this Friday. Would you consider babysitting Parker?"

"Of course!" Jade said. "We'd love to. We are so glad you met her."

He was, too. He'd survived weeks of physical therapy, attended a Sheffield Auto meeting with his dad and brothers. He'd even gone back to church. Going on a date couldn't be that big of a deal.

Anxiety knotted his gut. Dating. Did he even remember how to date anymore? And what if Celeste said no?

Celeste massaged the back of her neck and collapsed on the couch later that night. She'd finally finished her to-do list. She checked the clock. After nine. *Not bad.* It was the first time this week she'd finished before eleven. She hadn't had time to open the book she'd gotten from the library earlier, so reading tonight was her reward for wrapping up early.

She hoped this book would help her get her head on straight. It was time to overcome her infatuation with Sam, because having him act distant sliced her worse than any knife could.

The hot tea she'd brewed earlier had cooled, but she sipped it anyhow. Covering her legs with a plush cream blanket, she enjoyed the silence. Parker slept in his bedroom, and she'd tossed all his toys in a bin after putting him to bed, so the living room was neat, tidy. Home.

Her home—and it felt like home more than her old apartment. She'd been aimless there, just going with the flow of life, not following her dreams. Her dreams finally felt close, almost possible, living here in this pretty cabin on the lake.

Yawning, she reached for the book. *Lord, please open my heart to what I need to hear tonight.*

Two pages in, she hopped up and scurried to her small desk for a notebook. She wanted to remember the words, save them for when she had doubts. She returned, jotting notes as she studied the chapter. When she finished, she flipped back to review what she'd written.

When life doesn't pan out the way we imagined, we often blame ourselves. Life is full of surprises, some good, some bad. Accept them. Give thanks for them. Embrace the good surprises, and pray through the bad ones.

Pray through the bad? Did that imply the bad surprises would eventually end? She closed the notebook and clutched it to her chest.

God, please get me through the next week until my appointment. These scars were a bad surprise. Please change the doctor's mind. I want my old face back.

Her stomach coiled as she stared at the multicolored lights twinkling from the small tree she'd decorated and set up out of Parker's reach. Christmas—the time of hope.

Prayers were full of hope, too, so why didn't her prayer make her feel hopeful?

Random impressions flitted through her mind. Her mom's smile when she'd tucked Celeste's hair behind her ear on Thanksgiving. Dad's big hugs, the way he supported her decisions. The look in Sam's eyes when he called her beautiful.

Something niggled, and she didn't want to delve any deeper, but she couldn't deny reality—her prayer about having her old face back didn't leave her reassured. Maybe she needed to pray harder.

Her cell phone rang, shaking her out of her thoughts. She checked the caller, answering as soon as she saw Sam's name pop up.

"Hey, sorry to call so late." His voice reminded her of warm chocolate sauce, rich and decadent.

"I wasn't sleeping." Why did she sound like a chipmunk? She cleared her throat. "What's up?"

"I wanted to apologize for the bad mood I've been in. I shouldn't have taken it out on you."

He wasn't mad at her. She didn't fight the smile spreading across her face.

"Also I was wondering if you're free Friday night," he asked. "I want to take you out. On a date. We could get something to eat, go Christmas shopping or to a movie—whatever you want. Bryan and Jade will watch Parker for us, if you're okay with that."

He was asking her on a date—a real date!

"I would love to go. How about a toy store? I need to buy Parker's presents. I know what I want to get him, but I haven't had a chance to get out and purchase them."

"Sounds good. I'd say I would pick you up around six thirty, but you'll have to pick me up instead."

She laughed. "No problem. Six thirty it is."

That niggling doubt from earlier was nothing. She'd wanted a hopeful feeling, and Sam's call had more than accomplished it. She'd keep praying. The appointment would be a good surprise. It had to be.

Chapter Ten

Sam couldn't take his eyes off Celeste Friday night. She looked incredible in a deep red sweater, dark jeans and stylish boots. Her dark brown hair hung straight and shiny over her shoulders, and she wore eye makeup and red lipstick. They'd decided on an Italian restaurant, and after waiting thirty minutes for a table, they were finally sitting across from each other. With the exception of a few crying children, festive conversations filled the air. The right atmosphere to explore their relationship. Find out how she felt about some of the things on his mind.

The orders had been placed, and the salads had arrived. And his nerves were tighter than the compression sleeve he'd worn on his leg for months.

"How did Parker do last night?" Sam asked. "Are they still using him as baby Jesus?"

Celeste's smile took his breath away. Literally. An oxygen tank might be necessary.

"He did great. He was pretty tired, so Shelby kept him on her lap, and he didn't make a peep."

"Think he'll sit still on Christmas Eve?"

She shrugged, swirling her water with the straw. "I don't know. I hope so for Grandma Pearl's sake. I want her to be surprised, not embarrassed. I also don't want everyone thinking I'm a bad mom."

"You're a great mom." He wouldn't get a better lead-in than that. He leaned in. "Ever think about having more kids?"

She blinked, startled. "Sometimes."

"What do you mean?"

She fidgeted with her napkin. "I feel as if I'm in a grace period. This time in Lake Endwell—in Claire's cabin—has been wonderful, but it can't last forever."

"Why not?" He wasn't fool enough to believe it could, either, but why did she feel that way?

"It's not reality. A lot of my life is up in the air."

"I'm not following you." He pulled his shoulders back. Up in the air? Was she making plans he didn't know about?

"Well, a lot depends on my appointment this Thursday. If I hear good news, I'd like to start the process to get certified as a history teacher."

"What does your appointment have to do with that?"

Her chin dipped and her hair slid forward. "Everything. If I don't have scar reduction surgery, I don't see teaching in my future."

"You'd let that get in the way of your dream?"

"Well, *that* is a big deal to me." She straightened, one eyebrow raised. "I'm not up for the scrutiny. I can already guess the nickname the students would make up. 'Hey, there goes Scarface.'"

"They'll have a nickname for you no matter what. Kids always do. They would probably call me Limpy McGee."

"Yeah, well, I'll pass." She tossed the crumpled napkin on the table. "No, thank you."

"So, you'll keep doing your virtual assisting. No need for everything to change."

"Everything is changing soon, Sam. You know it. I know it."

He frowned. He did know it. Felt the change coming—couldn't deny it. The four walls of his life were shrinking in on him.

"You and I—we don't have to change." He waved his hand between them.

The corner of her mouth tweaked up. "I hope not, but you'll be back at work, and you'll see everything you missed. Life will be normal for you again."

"That's what I'm afraid of."

"What? You'll see everything you missed? Or life will be normal again?"

"Both. I *will* see everything I missed, and it will remind me I'll always miss some of it. Life doesn't really go back to normal. Not for me."

"Me, neither."

They didn't speak for a while. The waiter delivered steaming plates of pasta and a basket of bread, but they didn't dig in.

"Celeste? What kind of dad would Josh have been?"

"That's a tough question. He never met Parker. Never was around little kids that I can remember. I think he would have been wonderful. Maybe not the guy who volunteers to change a diaper, but he would have taught Parker how to ride a bike, and he would have played catch with him." Celeste twirled her fork in her pasta.

Her words didn't reassure him. Sam might not ever be able to teach a kid how to ride a bike or play catch with him.

"Do you ever worry about Parker not having a man

in his life? I mean, you're the one raising him. You're the biggest impact on his upbringing."

"I do worry. In fact, I feel terrible about it. I want him to have a father." She sighed. "My two best friends. Gone. Neither will know their son."

"That's why, when the time comes, Parker needs a dad who loves him." He selected a bread stick.

"I'm not thinking about any of that right now." Celeste blinked rapidly, her face stricken. "It's not as if I can pick up a dad in aisle six of the grocery store."

She wasn't thinking about any of that? "It's none of my business."

"I'm doing the best I can. Besides, no one is knocking down my door, desperate to be Parker's father."

What if someone did start knocking down her door? Someone other than him? "I'm not trying to make you mad. It's just, well, he's going to need a man in his life."

Celeste's jaw tightened. "I'm not going to date someone so Parker can have a father. I can't. I won't. I want more from marriage. And Parker has a grandpa who loves him very much. Until I find a man who loves both Parker and me with his whole heart, my dad will have to do." She shoved her chair back and marched in the direction of the restrooms.

Real smooth, Sheffield.

Why had he even brought the subject up? It wasn't as if he was in a position to be the man Parker or Celeste needed. Had he given her the impression he wanted her to find someone else?

He'd go after her, but the crutches...

Same old excuses. He hoisted himself to his feet and swung his way to the restroom hall. Felt stupid as a mom and two little girls passed him.

He waited.

Finally, Celeste opened the door.

"I'm sorry." Propping the right crutch against the wall, he took her hand and pulled her into a hug. She set her cheek on his shoulder. Her hair smelled flowery. He didn't care that they were in a restroom hallway in a crowded restaurant or that he was balancing on one foot.

She was in his arms. He stroked her hair with his free hand.

Celeste looked up at him. "Ever since our kiss last weekend, you've been giving me mixed signals."

"I know. I'm sorry. Let's talk about this at the table." They returned to their seats, and Sam waited for her to get comfortable. "I care about Parker. I want him to have a great life."

"I feel the same. I'm trying to give him one."

"I know. You're a terrific mother." The appreciation glowing in her face made him forget what he was going to say next.

Celeste tilted her head, watching his reaction. "You want kids, don't you?"

"Yeah, I do."

"You'll be a great dad."

Her confidence touched him. "Maybe someday. I can barely sign my name when I stand with these things—certainly can't change a diaper or carry a baby in my condition."

"You handle Parker pretty good now."

"Yeah, well, it's not the same. I mean, he's at my house. I want to take my kids to the soccer fields, throw them up in the air, put them on my shoulders."

"You can be a good dad and not do any of those things. I'd rather have a dad who loves me and never carries me on his shoulders than one who doesn't care."

He inwardly frowned. Yes, he could be a dad from

a wheelchair or crutches, but was that fair to Parker? Or Celeste? Not really. Celeste had so many problems. He wanted to provide solutions for her, not be one more problem. Maybe he'd been asking the wrong questions.

Trouble was, he wasn't ready to ask the right ones.

Later that evening, Celeste drove the minivan out of the mall parking lot and headed south to Lake Endwell. Stars dotted the black sky. What a beautiful night. Nothing could ruin this time with Sam. Thankfully, it wasn't snowing. "I still can't believe how many gifts you bought."

"What can I say? Big family." Even in the dim light, his smile sent sugarplums and Christmas wishes down to her boots.

The night had surprised and confused her, but after toy shopping for Parker, she and Sam were back to comfortable. She still wasn't completely sure why Sam had hounded her about dads during dinner, but at least they were talking again. And the darted glances Sam sent her all evening gave her the impression he liked her as much as she liked him.

He turned the radio on, flipping through the channels twice. "I guess we can't avoid Christmas music."

"Do you want to?"

"Nah. I love Christmas. What's your favorite song?"

She bit her lip as she thought about it. "Fast or slow?"

"Give me both."

"I love 'O Holy Night.' Gives me goose bumps every time I hear it. I've also always really liked 'Baby, It's Cold Outside.'"

He sang the opening line. She added the next one. They both laughed.

"What about you?" she asked. "What are your faves?"

"When I was a kid, I thought 'Grandma Got Run Over

by a Reindeer' was the funniest thing I'd ever heard. Drove my family nuts singing it all the time. I still like it."

"Me, too." She grinned.

"Would it be too cliché to admit 'Silent Night! Holy Night!' is another of my favorites?" He shifted to face her, and she had to fight to keep her eyes on the road.

"Of course not. It's beautiful. Classic. Everything Christmas should be."

The opening strains of "Grandma Got Run Over by a Reindeer" played on the radio. Sam began belting out the lyrics. "Come on, Celeste, join in."

He sang off-key and loud, but his exuberance infected her, so she sang, too. When the song ended, she laughed, breathless.

"A Holly Jolly Christmas" came on, and Sam sang in a ridiculously low voice.

Her mind blanked. Brandy's goofy face as they sang in the car last December swirled before her.

A night like this. With Christmas presents in the trunk. Joy-filled hearts.

Silly Christmas songs.

Taken from her, ripped from her.

Celeste's hands shook, her throat constricting, and she slowed, stopping the minivan on the side of the deserted country road. Her limbs felt ice-cold.

"What's wrong?" Sam craned his neck to see out her window, then his. "Is it the van?"

All she could do was give her head a tiny shake. A heavy sensation weighed her down like she'd been filled with concrete and it was hardening up.

"Celeste?" Sam's voice sounded far away…and worried. He shook her arm. "What's wrong? Are you okay?" He turned off the radio and grabbed his cell phone.

As soon as the music was cut, she snapped out of it. Sucked in a huge breath. Faced Sam.

"I don't know what happened, Sam. I'm sorry. I just… I heard the song and my whole body changed. I can't explain it. It was the same song we were singing when my car crashed last year." Her teeth chattered as a shiver overtook her. "This…this feels familiar in a terrible way."

"Hey…" He unbuckled his seat belt and scooted to her. Sneaked his hand behind her back and awkwardly pulled her to him with the armrests between them. He kissed her temple. "We're safe. Nothing is going to happen right now."

"You don't know that." She sniffed, easing back, but not far enough for him to drop his hand.

"We're safe."

"Brandy and I thought we were safe last year. We weren't. We're never safe. Never."

Sam inhaled, straightening his spine. "You're right. That was a stupid thing to say."

Regret at her outburst made her sit back. She didn't know what to think, what to do. She couldn't really say she was afraid to drive or that she believed she and Sam would be in a crash tonight. Something else had forced her to the side of the road.

Fear. But not fear of dying.

Fear of losing…again.

She couldn't handle the thought of losing Sam. She'd lost Brandy. And Josh.

Celeste exhaled loudly, avoiding looking at Sam. "Let's go home."

"Wait." He touched the back of her hand. "Stay here a minute. I'm not in a hurry."

Her throat felt as if she'd swallowed acid. She brought

her hands to her face, closing her eyes. She was acting like an idiot—a drama queen. Why was she so worked up? She'd driven hundreds of times since the accident. This wasn't her first go-round in a vehicle with Sam, either.

And he wasn't hers to lose.

God, I need You. I don't know what to pray for, but I need You.

"You've faced your fears, Celeste. Moved. Figured out a new job. Driven past the crash site. I haven't even gone back to my dealership." Sam's voice soothed her agitation. "How do you do it? Like tonight, you're driving. It's almost the anniversary of the accident, but you got the courage to go out there."

"Courage?" She barked a dry laugh. "This isn't courageous. My hands are still shaking."

"But you're here." He faced her again, his face intense in the dim light.

Why was she here? How could she answer him?

"I guess I didn't consider the similarities between tonight and last year. Maybe I should have."

"You still would have come," he said. "You're a fighter."

"I'm no fighter. I'm more of a drifter. Responding to what life gives me."

"That's not true."

She wanted to believe him, but her track record showed the truth. She'd never had the courage—even before the accident—to even decide what her dreams were, let alone pursue them. If she had, she'd have been teaching history all this time instead of working at dead-end jobs.

So what did she want now?

She covered Sam's hand with hers. *I don't want to lose you, Sam. But I don't know what to do about it.*

His thumb brushed hers. He pulled her into a hug, and she rested her cheek on his shoulder. A strong man to lean on—her dream guy come true.

Love. Commitment. A family.

But what if he wasn't ready for all that?

Fighting wasn't her strong suit, and right now her energy was drained. Empty. It was easier to drift along, taking what life gave.

She hoped she wouldn't have to fight for all the things she still wanted, most of all, him.

She didn't know if she had enough fight in her. She needed something easy right now.

Chapter Eleven

Sunday morning after church, Sam shoveled a forkful of hash browns into his mouth at Pat's Diner. Dad, chugging coffee and eyeing a piece of bacon, sat across from him. The sermon this morning had brought up some questions. About work. About Celeste. About his faith.

Maybe Dad could help.

"I'm starting to see why you haven't been out much." Dad clunked his coffee cup on the table. "Is everyone always this bad?"

Sam finished chewing and grinned. "Worse. This is actually light compared to what Celeste and I deal with at the grocery store."

Dad shook his head. "It's not like you were abducted by aliens. You were in an accident. And why did the Swanson kid ask if you saw a bright light?"

Sam shrugged, slurping his coffee. "You know his mom. Probably took him to see one of those I-died-and-went-to-heaven movies. It's all right. No harm done."

"It's annoying."

"I've gotten used to it." Sam soaked in the atmosphere. It was good to be back here. Pat's Diner had been a staple in his life for as long as he could remember. The red vinyl seats of the booth squeaked with each movement. Conversation hummed around them. Outside the large window, snow fell in big flakes over the sidewalk. Trees had been strung with lights for the big parade Saturday.

"Dr. Stepmeyer wants me to talk to Dr. Curtis before I go back to work." Sam flexed his right knee slightly.

"I figured that was a given."

"Yeah, well, I hadn't been planning on it."

"You should." Dad bit into the bacon.

"Nah, I'm ready."

Dad paused midchew and gave him the look, the one only his dad could give.

Twenty-seven and Sam still squirmed at that look. He diverted his attention to the stack of pancakes in front of him. After Celeste had dropped him off Friday night, he'd spent hours sitting in the living room with just the Christmas tree lights on. He'd been thinking. About Celeste and how brave she was. About how he'd been avoiding life instead of meeting it face-on the way she did.

He was ready. Ready for work. Ready for more.

And he needed to figure out today's sermon.

"Dad, did you ever feel that God didn't care about you?" Sam focused on Dad's reaction.

He set his mug down gently this time. Rubbed his chin. "I'm not going to lie. Yes. I felt that way for a long time."

"After Mom died?"

"No—before."

Sam sputtered, not expecting those words. "What? Why?"

Dad slid his plate to the side and clasped his hands

to rest on the table. "I'm not proud of this, so I hope you don't judge me too hard."

His dad? Less than perfect? Not possible.

"I won't. I couldn't. You're… Just tell me."

"Your mom and I married pretty young. I was going to college to be an architect. Before either of us knew it, she was pregnant with Tom."

Sam nodded, sipping his coffee.

"I couldn't support her and a family *and* go to college for two more years, so I dropped out. Went to work for my dad."

Sam had always known Dad hadn't finished college, but he'd never really thought about the circumstances.

"I hated it at first. Loved Tom and your mother, but I resented that my dreams had to die. I stopped going to church. I told myself God didn't care or He would have made a way for me to finish school."

"What changed your mind? What brought you back to church?"

Dad smiled. "Your mother. She was something." He stared out the window, a faraway look in his eyes. "When Tom started walking, I decided enough was enough. I was going back to college and finishing my degree. It's not that I hated working for my dad—I didn't mind, not really—but I wanted my way. Wanted life to be my way. So I gathered my courage and marched into our little brick house after work one night, ready to tell your mother I was quitting my job and finishing school."

"Did she get mad or something?" Sam tried to picture them, but he couldn't. The only memories he had of his mom weren't his—just stories and photographs passed down from his siblings.

"No. She was standing over the stove, crying her eyes out." His face fell. "She seemed so devastated. I forgot everything, just rushed over and took her into my arms. I was scared, I'll tell you that."

"Why was she crying?"

The most tender expression Sam had ever seen spread across Dad's face. "She handed me a pregnancy test. We were having another baby."

Sam was taken aback. "Didn't she want one?"

"Let me finish the story." Dad lifted his finger. "When she calmed down enough to speak, she told me she knew I was miserable. She'd been scrimping on groceries and expenses so I could go back to school. She opened a cupboard and pulled down a coffee can. Handed it to me, saying, 'There's sixty-seven dollars in here. I thought we could get by if you went back to school, but with another baby on the way…'"

Sam's heart tugged at his mom's generosity. She must have loved Dad very much.

"In that moment, I changed. I completely changed. I'd been thinking about me and what I wanted, not realizing how blessed I was to have her love and her children. I silently asked God to forgive me. Wrapped her in my arms and told her I was opening my own dealership— my dad had wanted me to anyhow—and she wouldn't have to worry about money. It took some convincing, but she eventually believed me."

"Should she have?" The words were out before Sam could think about them. But he wanted to know—had Dad meant those words?

"Yes." He leveled an honest stare at Sam. "She absolutely should have believed me, because I meant it. Sheffield Auto wasn't my dream, at least not then, but *she* was. And I knew I had to embrace her and our growing family or we'd both be miserable. I'm proud of my years with our company, and God gave me a second chance at a career of my choosing when he sent Reed to Lake Endwell. I love being his superintendent. Building houses is even better than designing them."

Sam hadn't realized Dad had sacrificed so much for them.

"I've been mad at God for not healing me." Just saying those words twisted Sam's gut.

"We're all thankful you're alive. You don't know how bad it was for all of us the night of your accident. I've never been more scared in my life."

There was truth in those words, Sam knew it. But…

"You're my son, Sam. I love you. I couldn't handle losing you. I still can't. So you can be mad at whomever you want, including God, but every day I praise Him for keeping you here. If you can't praise Him for saving you, maybe you can thank Him for answering *my* prayer. Because I'd be a shell of a man if I'd have lost you, too."

Emotion welled in Sam's chest, and he had to bow his head. "I never really thought about how my accident affected you."

"It's okay. I didn't think about how my resentment affected your mom. But when I did…" Dad sipped his coffee.

"You put her first."

"Love will do that to you."

"Thanks for telling me this, Dad."

"I love you. Never forget it."

He wouldn't. Couldn't. He'd taken his family for granted, been caught up in his own problems.

"I love you, too, Dad."

Well, God, I'm doing like Dad said—Thank You for answering his prayer and saving me. I'm not thrilled about my disabilities, but I'm thankful to be here.

Another thought came uninvited.

Maybe Sam was too focused on wanting his way, just like Dad had been too focused years ago.

A wave of guilt hit him. He kept thinking about himself. He'd taken Celeste out the other night, made her uncomfortable with his intrusive comments about Parker needing a dad and hadn't put two and two together about her accident until it was too late and she was crying at the side of the road. He counted on his leg healing, but even then he might not be the guy she needed.

If he could just tell that to his heart…

"This blanket is so soft, dear." Grandma Pearl beamed. A quiet Sunday afternoon, perfect for Celeste to visit the assisted living complex and drop off an early Christmas present. "How did you know I can never get warm enough?"

"I'm glad you like it. It's hard to stay warm this time of year." Celeste turned the page of the storybook for Parker, sitting on her lap. Her heart broke a little at how frail Grandma Pearl looked lately. "Are you feeling okay? Want me to get you some tea?"

"I'm better. Had a cold last week. I'm happy watching Parker. He's a smart one, isn't he?"

"He is. Takes after Brandy."

"He's got a good mama teaching him."

Celeste didn't respond. She'd made her peace with Parker calling her Mama but she still wished his real mama was here. Grandma Pearl wouldn't be around forever, either. Why did people have to die?

"One of my friends from church stopped by yesterday." Grandma Pearl unfolded the blanket and smoothed it over her lap. "She told me she saw you with a young man. Tell me about him."

Here we go. What could she say? "Um, yes, Sam is

the man I mentioned on Thanksgiving. The one who lives next door."

"Sam. That's a lovely name. I knew a Sam way back when."

She nodded, hoping Grandma Pearl would hop right back on memory lane so Celeste wouldn't have to talk about him.

"Is he a keeper?"

"Um, well…"

"Is he a Christian?"

"Yes."

"For years my Stanley never wanted to go to church with me. I could barely get him to the Christmas service, even when our Joanie—that's Brandy's mom, you know—sang with her Sunday school class. One year—Joanie must have been seven or eight—she looked at me and told me she wasn't going to church anymore."

Celeste fought back a smile.

"Well, I didn't know what to do. Joanie had always been such a good girl. I told her she most certainly was going to church, and she said, 'Daddy never goes, so I'm not going, either.'"

She bit her lower lip.

"I didn't have time to pray on it, because Stanley stormed into the room and said we were all going to church. And he did. From then on, we went as a family. He might not have ever showed it much, but he was a God-fearing man. I was blessed to be married to him."

Parker climbed off Celeste's lap and toddled over to Grandma Pearl's. "If your legs hurt, you don't have to hold him…"

"Nonsense. I want nothing more than to hold this precious baby in my arms. We're the last ones of the family. Joanie died when Brandy was a teenager. Stanley passēd a few years later. And Brandy…" Her eyes welled with tears. She gently brushed them away. "Well, I'm thankful this sweet boy will carry on. A little part of me, a little part of Stanley. Joanie and Brandy. He's got a bit of all of us."

It was true. Celeste saw glimpses of Brandy in the way he held his head when deep in thought. And she saw Josh in Parker's big smile.

"Grandma Pearl?"

"What, dear?"

"Do you ever worry about Parker? I mean, do you worry about me raising him?"

Grandma Pearl's papery cheeks lifted as she smiled. "No. I'm thankful you're raising him. I know you'll love him the way Brandy would. The only time I fret is when I think of his father."

"Josh?"

"No. The man you'll marry someday. I worry he won't love Parker the way he would his own child. But whenever I worry, I give it to God. He's gotten me through a lot of losses. I trust He'll lead you to the right man."

"You pray for me?" Celeste was touched.

"Of course I do. I pray for Parker and for you and for the man who will complete your family. I love you."

"I love you, too." Celeste looked away, emotional at her thoughtfulness.

"Tell me more about this Sam who lives next door. Think he might be the one?"

Heat climbed her neck. "I'd like him to be, but I don't know."

"What don't you know?"

"He's not ready for a family."

Her face fell. "That's too bad, dear. I was hoping for your sake and mine he would like Parker."

"I think he loves Parker. It's just…well, he was in a bad accident, and his leg might never heal all the way."

"Does that bother you?"

"No. Not at all. He's wonderful with Parker, and I like him a lot."

"So he's nervous about his leg."

That about summed it up.

Celeste shrugged. "I'm nervous, too." Parker had relaxed on Grandma Pearl's lap and rubbed his eyes. Celeste handed him a sippy cup.

"What are you nervous about?"

Celeste pointed at her forehead and her cheek.

"The scars? They could never take away from your beauty. Your soul shines through. That's the real beauty, you know."

She wished the sweet woman was right. She stood and bent over Grandma Pearl to give her a hug. "I love you."

"I love you, too, dear." She kissed the top of Parker's head. "The right man for you will never think less of you because of your scars. He'll see the best in you. Always."

Sam had never acted like her scars were an issue. He'd even called her beautiful. But maybe he'd been trying to make her comfortable. He might not have really meant it.

Four more days and she'd have a verdict about her face.

Maybe it wouldn't matter if Sam meant it or not. With more surgery, she'd be the girl she used to be. Except better. After her face healed, she was going to be the woman she should have been all along.

Chapter Twelve

"Are you sure you don't want us to come with you?" Sam stood next to Celeste as she set the diaper bag on his table Thursday morning. He wanted to ease her worry about today's doctor's appointment, but how could he? Celeste's pale face looked exhausted. Had she gotten any sleep last night?

"No, thank you." She smoothed her hair behind her ear. "Don't take this personally, but I'd rather go alone."

He propped a crutch against the table and took her hand. Cold. She must be nervous. "I understand."

"It's just a consultation."

With most of his weight on his left leg, Sam drew her closer and touched her chin directly below her lips. She flinched. Was it him? "I'm sorry."

"It's not you… It's the nerve ending there. Whenever I touch that spot, it stings."

He dropped his hand to his side and his attention to the floor. He'd seen her smart at times when she touched her face. He should have remembered.

"Are you sure you can handle him for a few hours?" Celeste searched the room, settling her gaze on Parker banging a plastic hammer against Sam's coffee table.

Sam had asked himself the same thing. But he'd never had a problem watching Parker while Celeste ran, and what was another hour? He could always use the wheelchair if he needed both hands to change a diaper or pick Parker up.

"I've got this. And Aunt Sally is home." Sam had talked to his aunt last night, and she'd assured him she'd be home if he needed her. "She lives two miles away. If I have any trouble, she'll be here at the snap of my fingers."

"Okay. I'd better get going." Celeste pivoted to leave. "Don't want to be late."

"Celeste?" He prepared to follow her. He had so many things he wanted to say. She didn't need to worry. Surgery or no surgery, she was stunning, breathtaking. The woman who had made him want to live again. The one he owed so much to, the only woman he had eyes for. The one he'd told himself was off-limits. Who deserved more in a man than he could give. But the words dried up before he could say them. "Call me when the appointment is over."

She nodded and left.

Sunshine spilled to the deck. The weatherman had announced a high of thirty-four degrees Fahrenheit today. Fitting, since Christmas was next week. He hoped the parade on Saturday would be warmer.

He'd been anticipating the parade ever since the day he'd offered to take Celeste. And it was almost here. He wouldn't even need a wheelchair for the event. For some reason getting around town on crutches didn't bother him the way the wheelchair did. She'd told him her parents were babysitting Parker for the day, so it would be just the two of them.

"Dada." Parker pointed at Sam.

His heart stopped beating. Had Parker called him…?

"Dada." Parker ran to Sam and stretched his arms up.

Emotion swelled, puffing Sam's chest out at the wonder of those two syllables.

What if he was Parker's daddy?

That would mean… He gulped. Taking his relationship with Celeste to a level he'd refused to consider up to this point.

If he'd never been in the accident, he would have pursued Celeste from day one. With or without Parker. He liked how he felt when he was with her. He liked her smile and the way she made him want to be a better person. He liked the kisses she showered on Parker's cheeks. He liked her courage and tenacity. She worked hard and expected little.

And that was exactly what she would get if he pursued her now. Hard work and little to show for it.

He wasn't husband material. He wasn't father material, either.

But, oh, how he wanted it. All of it. Celeste and Parker were the family he wanted.

Had he fallen in love with her?

"Dada."

"Hey, little buddy, I'll pick you up, but I have to sit first." Sam headed to the couch. After he settled in, he patted his lap for Parker to join him. Parker toddled over, and Sam picked him up, hugging him tightly, breathing in his baby smell, and tucked him onto his lap. "What should we do while your mommy is at her appointment? Want me to read you a story?"

Sam stretched to grab the pile of picture books Stephanie had dropped off a few days ago. He opened one about a bunny all alone at Christmas. Parker helped turn the pages. Good thing they were made of heavy coated cardboard, otherwise the kid might have ripped them. After the first book, Sam read another. Parker got bored, so he helped him off his lap. He ran straight for the plastic hammer, and once more, he banged it on the coffee table.

Maybe Parker would build houses when he grew up. Sam's brother-in-law Reed could hire him. Sam smiled at the thought.

He turned the television to a cartoon and swung over to the table to find a snack for Parker. The diaper bag revealed wipes, half a dozen diapers, baby pain reliever, a thermometer, several plastic toys, a sealed bag with animal crackers, containers of baby food—no prunes, thankfully—and three changes of clothes. Celeste had left two sippy cups in the fridge. She certainly was prepared. He slung a tote bag over his shoulder, put the crackers in it and walked to the kitchen. He kept his crutch secure as he slipped one of the cups in his bag. Then he returned to the living room.

A quick once-over didn't reveal Parker. Sam frowned, searching for him.

There, behind the Christmas tree. Parker crawled around under the tree, snagging the tree skirt.

"No, Parker!" All he could envision was the tree toppling on the baby. "Come here."

Parker paused, staring at Sam through startled eyes that began to fill with tears. "Waah!"

As his wail picked up volume, Sam debated his next move. He needed to get him out from under the Christmas tree to keep him safe. But if he took the time to get into the wheelchair, Parker could try to pull himself up by a branch or break a glass bulb and get cut or...

What should he do? His brain froze. His body did, too. Parker rocked back and forth on all fours, crying loudly.

"Come out here," he said in what he hoped was a soothing tone. Sam hopped as close as he could with the crutches and tried to bend. "Let's get a snack, buddy. I've got crackers."

Parker didn't crawl out. Instead, he shifted backward, his head hitting the bottom branches of the artificial tree in the process. Two felt reindeer, a candy cane and a glass bulb hit the ground. His cries grew even louder.

Sam heaved a sigh of relief that the bulb didn't break. He turned quickly, knowing he needed to get into his wheelchair so he could salvage this. But as soon as he took two steps, Parker crawled out, howling at the top of his lungs. The boy stood, stumbled toward Sam and tripped, hitting his forehead on the edge of the wooden dining chair near the tree.

Sam watched in horror as Parker bounced off the edge of the chair, falling backward and smacking the back of his skull on the hardwood floor. Sam lunged forward, dropping his right crutch and instinctively trying to bear weight on his right leg so he could pick up Parker. But the knee wasn't strong enough, and his right leg collapsed beneath him, sending him sprawling on his side.

Pain ripped up his thigh. He clutched the leg as he inched his way to Parker. An angry purple goose egg had already formed on the baby's forehead. His cries were hysterical. Waves of helplessness crashed over Sam as he writhed in pain, wanting more than anything to take Parker in his arms and assess how badly the child was hurt.

Sam pushed himself to his elbows, dragging himself to the end table where he'd left his phone. He speed-dialed his aunt.

* * *

The paper crinkled as Celeste shifted on the examination table. Dr. Smith typed notes on the laptop. He hadn't said much as he examined her. The questions had all been expected. No surprises there.

The only surprise would be his verdict.

Yes?

No?

She wanted yes.

How she wanted yes.

Dr. Smith swiveled on the stool. "You've healed remarkably well. The scars are flat, with the exception of the slightly raised one above your left temple. They've faded nicely."

Celeste's pulse raced, ticking as furiously as a bomb about to detonate.

"So what does that mean?" She wrung her hands together, daring to hope. And trying not to hope. "I can get more surgery?"

He frowned, shaking his head. "You don't need more surgery."

Didn't need more surgery? The ocean roared in her head, and a tidal wave drowned out all thoughts.

She *did* need more surgery.

Didn't he understand? Didn't he get it?

"The nerve endings are too damaged for two of your scars, but the other ones could benefit from…" The doctor droned on but he might as well have been speaking gibberish.

She'd have to look like this the rest of her life. Have to face the reminders of that night every time she glanced in the mirror.

"…the treatment I recommend…" His voice sounded far away, in another county, another life.

She wanted to laugh—let out a high-pitched scream. She'd applied the silicone gel sheets for months. Massaged the prescribed ointment into the scars for as long as the doctor ordered. Still lathered on vitamin E cream before bed. Whatever *treatment* he recommended was not going to make these lines disappear.

"Why?" She cut him off. "Why can't I have more surgery?"

He took a deep breath. "Celeste, more surgery wouldn't help. I don't think you understand what I'm saying."

Wouldn't help? Did this guy have any idea how much this meant to her?

Her cell phone rang. She set it to silence. It vibrated over and over, and frustrated, she yanked it to see who was calling.

Sally.

"Hello?"

"Celeste, hon, I don't want to worry you, but Parker took a little tumble, and Sam did, too, so I'm at the ER to make sure they're okay. Parker has an ugly bump on his forehead, but he's sipping some milk and I've got him calmed down."

Her heart stopped beating. "And Sam?"

"I'm not sure."

Oh, no. Oh, no.

Parker. Sam.

"I'll be right there." She clicked End, sliding off the examination table, ripping the paper she'd been sitting on in the process. Parker needed her. Sam needed her. "I've got to go. My son…"

"I hope everything is all right."

"Me, too." She clutched her purse and opened the door.

"Wait. Take these pamphlets about the laser treatment I just outlined."

She wasn't interested in anything except her guys right now. She swiped the pamphlets Dr. Smith held and marched out of the room, down the hall and outside to the parking lot.

Forcing herself not to freak out about Parker, Sam or her diagnosis, she sped all the way to the hospital. Maybe if she drove fast enough, the pain stabbing her heart would vanish. If she could, she'd drive all the way back to last year, before the accident. She'd cancel her and Brandy's plans. Reschedule their shopping date. Then Brandy would still be here, and Celeste wouldn't have to worry about living with her scars, Parker being hurt or Sam not walking.

She'd gotten too close. She couldn't bear it if Sam was badly injured. And what about Parker? What could the side effects of bumping his head lead to?

God, take care of them.

"The good news is you don't need surgery." Dr. Curtis refastened the ice pack wrap around Sam's knee, which had swollen considerably. "Your quads weren't strong enough to support your weight and that's why your leg buckled. The ligaments aren't torn. The X-rays show no broken bones, and other than some muscle strain, your knee should be fine."

Sam could barely think about his leg right now. Aunt Sally had texted Sam and told him she thought Parker would be okay. Just a bump on the head. She couldn't come up yet, because she was waiting for Celeste to arrive. The hospital needed Celeste's authorization to treat Parker. And, yes, Sally had called her.

Sam ground his teeth together. Aunt Sally wasn't a doctor. She might think it was a bump, but what did she know? Why wouldn't the doctors look at the kid? Why did they have to wait for Celeste? Parker could have a concussion. Bleeding on the brain.

What if Sam's negligence caused Parker long-term damage?

"The test results were promising. You still have good reactivation in your leg muscles, but the electrical signals passing through the nerve don't have the speed we're hoping for. There is also mild inflammation in there." Dr. Curtis folded his hands.

"What does that mean?" Sam tried to sit up. Dr. Curtis pressed the button for the bed to rise.

"It means your mobility depends on continuing physical therapy and protecting your leg at all costs. When you tore the ACL in June, it set you back. In my professional opinion, it's unlikely you'll restore full range of motion in your right knee. My guess is seventy-five degrees. That doesn't mean you won't have a functional leg. You're young and healthy. The more therapy you do, the more strength you'll regain."

"What does 'functional' mean? You're saying I won't walk normally, is that it?"

"Your chances weren't good after the boating accident. A torn ACL didn't improve them. Do I think it's possible you'll need to use a cane when you leave the house? Yes. If you're diligent about strength training and PT. Who knows? Another year from now, you might surprise me by walking in on both feet unassisted."

"Why am I sensing a *but*?" Dread dropped in his gut.

"The knee injury compromised your recovery. It's hard to make a knee stable. You were already at a disadvantage to begin with. Healthy patients with torn ACLs struggle to completely heal. Protecting your leg—your knee especially—must be your top priority. I'm not talking weeks. I'm talking months. Years."

Sam tried to take it all in. He knew he couldn't reinjure the leg or knee again. It might permanently disable him, and he couldn't face the not knowing, the uncertainty of another operation. Another fall could put an end to his dream of walking unassisted. But what about his other dreams?

"It's been almost eighteen months since I've worked. I planned on returning in January."

"Remind me again what you do." The doctor took a seat in the chair next to the bed, his white lab coat spilling to the sides.

"I own an auto dealership." Sam shifted his jaw. "I'm on my feet a lot."

Dr. Curtis locked eyes with Sam's. "Last time I saw you, you weren't walking at all due to the pain."

"I'm still in pain. But I've been using crutches for over a month now."

"Yes." He clicked a pen. "And here we are."

Frustrated, Sam let his head fall back to the pillow. "You and Dr. Stepmeyer are the ones who wanted me out of the wheelchair."

"We still do. But we also want you to be smart. You weren't wearing your brace when you arrived. I know you can bear a limited amount of weight on your right leg, but until your quads can bear your full weight, you need the brace."

"So can I go to work or not?" He sounded annoyed. He knew it. Couldn't help it. He *was* annoyed. Desperate, even.

"It depends." Dr. Curtis pulled his laptop to him. "I think returning to work is possible, but only if you take it easy. Consider part-time for the first couple of months. Expect it to be exhausting, and don't be a hero. Crutches are unstable under ideal conditions. An oil-soaked shop floor and an outdoor car lot during a Michigan winter are not ideal. My advice is to use your wheelchair in the shop and outdoors when it's snowing, raining or icy. Only use crutches on non-slippery surfaces. I'm sure I don't need to tell you this, but if you overuse your leg, it will swell. Keep an ice wrap on site. Most of all, remember what I said—protect the knee."

The advice hit home, but Sam didn't want to acknowledge the truth. He glanced at his swollen leg encased in a hefty black brace. He'd better tell the doctor everything. "I wasn't planning on bringing the wheelchair to work."

The doctor looked up from typing on his laptop and sighed. "Do you want to schedule the knee surgery now? Because one more slip with the crutches and you'll be bedridden. Again. I don't think you realize how fortunate you were to avoid tearing anything today. We could be in surgery right this minute."

Sam let it sink in.

Unrealistic—that was what he'd been. The doctor was right. Why had he thought he'd go back to working a full shift on crutches when he could only put a fraction of his weight on his bad leg? And the shop floor *was* slippery. It would be stupid to attempt hobbling around on crutches through it.

"Do you have any other questions?" Dr. Curtis stood.

Sam shook his head. The doctor nodded and said goodbye.

It was sheer arrogance to think he could resume life on his terms just because he wanted to. Forget returning to work. He'd told himself over and over he wouldn't go back there in a wheelchair. And he'd been wrong to babysit Parker today. He couldn't handle a toddler. He cringed remembering how the little guy had crawled under the Christmas tree when Sam turned his back. The way he'd run after Sam. Hitting his head.

My fault.

Sam closed his eyes, his heart burning.

He wasn't fit for work. He certainly wasn't fit for taking care of a child.

And now Celeste would know it, too. The huge purple bump on Parker's forehead was proof enough. Sam wouldn't blame her for seeing him for what he really was—incapable. He'd been right all along. Celeste deserved someone who could take care of her, someone who would shoulder the care of their children, who could carry groceries for her and drive a car.

He was not that man. It was time to put her needs first, which meant stepping away. Even if it destroyed him.

Chapter Thirteen

Celeste raced through the sliding doors of the hospital, halting at the information desk. Her mind hadn't stopped spitting out nightmare scenarios since Sally called. What if Parker had gotten worse? What if Sam had broken his leg?

After being directed to the waiting room, she scurried down the hallway and spotted Sally rocking Parker. Celeste slowed to catch her breath. "How is he?"

Sally looked up and smiled. "Almost asleep. He took a hard hit to the noggin. The nurse gave me an ice pack." She held up a round gel pack shaped like a frog. "I'll hold him while you check him in."

"Thank you. I'll be right back." Celeste pushed her hair back behind her ear. The waiting room looked inviting with sage-green chairs, a television and a large fish tank. It was also surprisingly quiet. Only a handful of chairs were occupied. Maybe she wouldn't have to wait long for them to treat Parker. After talking to a nurse, she filled out paperwork and returned. She lifted Parker out of Sally's arms, kissing the purple bump on his forehead.

"Mama," he murmured, wrapping his arms around her neck.

"You poor thing. Looks like you got an owie." A double-chocolate, frosted brownie couldn't be sweeter than this boy. She hugged him tight and met Sally's eyes. "Have you heard from Sam?"

"He was waiting to get test results last I heard."

"Do you think he tore anything? Broke anything?" Celeste moved Parker so he was sitting on her lap. She gently felt around his skull, finding a bump on the back of his head, too. Parker seemed okay. They'd find out for sure as soon as a doctor could see him. But Sam? Fear twisted in her abdomen.

"I don't know." Sally's kind eyes dimmed. "I hope not. He's been through enough."

Celeste agreed. He'd been through so much. Why did he have to fall? Today of all days. They were supposed to be going to the Christmas parade Saturday. It was all she'd looked forward to since he'd asked her to go with him. It was unlikely he'd be able to go now.

"Thank you for taking care of Parker until I could get here."

Sally patted Celeste's hand. "I'm glad I could, hon. I love babies. Parker is a sweetheart, and I'd do anything for Sam."

She would do anything for Sam, too. She loved him. And it was eating her alive not knowing if he'd seriously hurt his leg. He'd made so much progress since she'd met him.

Dear Lord, please let Sam be okay. Keep his leg safe. Heal him. Comfort him.

"What are your Christmas plans?" Sally asked.

"Parker is going to be baby Jesus in a children's service at his mom's old church." Celeste frowned. "I should call the director and tell her Parker won't be at practice tonight. I'm sure he's had enough excitement today."

Sally gestured to her. "Go ahead. If you're like me, you'll forget to do it later."

Celeste called Sue Roper and told her Parker wouldn't be there. Then, as she chatted with Sally about the Sheffield Christmas traditions, Lake Endwell and the big parade, she began to calm down. Parker rested on her lap, and before they knew it, an hour had passed.

"Parker Monroe," a nurse called.

Celeste gave Sally a shaky smile. "We'll be back. Please let me know as soon as you hear anything from Sam."

"I'm not going anywhere. I'll shoot you a text if I get any news."

"Thank you."

She and Parker followed a nurse to an examination room. Forty-five minutes later, Parker was given the all clear, and Celeste held instructions about warning signs after a head injury. He started fussing, so she bought a package of crackers from a vending machine before returning to where Sally sat.

"He's being released." Sally slid her phone into her purse as Celeste approached. "He'll be right down."

Overcome with relief, Celeste fell into a chair, ripped open the crackers and handed the bag to Parker. "He must be okay if they're releasing him."

"Praise the good Lord." Sally closed her eyes a moment. "That boy will be the death of me. I've never worried about anyone as much as I have him the last eighteen months."

"I know what you mean. He's pretty special."

"He is." Sally pushed herself up from the chair, her

eyes suspiciously watery. "I'm going to find a pop machine and get my sugar and caffeine on. Be right back."

Celeste smoothed Parker's hair from his forehead as Sally disappeared. What a day. She still hadn't processed her own doctor's visit, and here she was, dealing with Parker's and wondering how Sam had fared.

She glanced down the hall. Someone in scrubs pushed Sam in a wheelchair. Her heart did a backflip. The grim expression on his face worried her, though. Had he gotten terrible news? Was he in pain?

She carried Parker, munching on his snack, toward him. Sam said something to the man pushing him, and the man patted his shoulder then left. Sam wheeled himself the rest of the way.

"Dada!" Parker squirmed, twisting so both arms reached for Sam. She caught her breath. Had Parker just called Sam Dad? It sounded so right.

But Sam didn't look happy. He didn't take Parker in his arms. In fact, his face drained of color.

"Did they run tests?" Sam asked. "Is Parker going to be okay?"

"He'll be fine." She patted her purse. "I have a list of things to watch for, but I'm more worried about you. Are you all right?"

He nodded curtly.

"What did the doctor say?" She gestured to his leg, but he didn't meet her eyes.

"Nothing I didn't already know."

His dead tone and the way his gaze locked to the wall raised the hair on her arms.

"Tell me what's wrong." She touched his hand. He flinched, snatching it back.

"Nothing's wrong. How did your appointment go?" His question had no feeling behind it.

She wanted to lie, to tell him it went great, that a few months from now he'd see her at her best, scar-free. But this was Sam. He'd become her safe place. The man she could be honest with, the one who made her feel comfortable, happy again.

"The doctor won't do more surgery." All her hopes leaked out at each word. *Please let this not change anything. Let me be wrong. Maybe living with my scars isn't as bad as I thought.*

The muscle in his cheek ticked. "So, lousy news all around."

He still wouldn't make eye contact. And his reaction? Confusing.

What had she expected? *Comfort. A hug. Maybe even, in my wildest dreams, for him to say, "It doesn't matter. You're flawless in my eyes."*

But she wasn't flawless. Would never be flawless.

Sam rubbed his thigh where the brace ended. "I shouldn't have babysat Parker. I won't make that mistake again. And don't worry—I'll find someone else to drive me to my appointments."

Her head reeled. Find someone else? Why? Had he been banking on her being scar-free, too? Before her head exploded with worries, she inhaled. No sense guessing. She'd ask him instead.

"Why would you find someone else to drive you?"

"I was forcing something."

"What are you talking about?"

"I wanted my life to be different." He put his fist to his lips, turning his head to the side. "I was wrong. I accept that."

Was he speaking in some weird code? She tried to decipher his words, his attitude. "Is this about my scars or your leg?"

He shrugged. "Both, I guess. We want to erase our accidents, but we can't."

Both. Her scars *were* a factor.

"What aren't you saying?" Her voice rose, sounded screechy to her ears. "Why now? You reinjured your leg, didn't you? Is it permanent?"

"This isn't about my leg." He finally met her eyes. "It's about you. And me. And reality."

If it wasn't his leg, it must be her scars. She had the sensation ice was freezing her body from her toes up her torso to her neck and head. "What changed?"

"Nothing. And that's the problem. I thought my situation had changed, but it didn't. If we don't put an end to this now, we'll end up hurt."

Too late. She was in too deep.

"I don't understand," she said. "I thought we had something…"

"I'm sorry if I led you on."

Led her on? Her throat was closing in. She fought for breath. Jostled Parker as she willed her legs to support her.

"I see," she said. "So you don't want me around at all, is that it? You don't need my help. What about the parade?"

He shook his head, his lips drawing together tightly, virtually disappearing. "It's for the best."

The words were a verbal slap to the face. Her heartbeat slowed, her blood turning to sludge. He'd obviously made up his mind. They—whatever *they* were—no longer existed. He didn't want her.

There was nothing left to do but leave.

"I suppose you heard all that?" Sam yanked the wheels to get through the hospital hallway as quickly as possible.

Aunt Sally half jogged at his side. He'd done the right thing. Let Celeste go. She could find someone worthy of her, someone who would protect her and Parker.

Given his limitations, it was a crime to chain her to him. He would just bring more problems to her life. Celeste's life was full of problems already.

If he could get his heart to listen… It was clenching, bleeding, wringing itself into a tiny ball of nothing.

He'd had it all for a brief moment. Hope. The hope of the life he wanted. But reality collided with fantasy, and it was over.

"I tried to give you two some privacy, but your body language said it all." Aunt Sally made a clucking sound. "I don't know what is going on with you, but I don't like this."

"You don't know anything about it."

"I know Celeste has the patience of Mother Teresa. She's good for you. She was worried, and from the look on her face when she hightailed it out of here, I'd say you just broke her heart."

"I did her a favor." The cold air smacked his cheeks as he rolled onto the sidewalk. He stopped near the side of the entrance where he could wait for Aunt Sally to drive the car around. "I want to go home."

"Well, too bad, Sam." Flames shot from her eyes as she planted her hands on her hips directly in front of him. "You've gotten your way ever since the accident, and you know what? Today you don't get to have your way. You're going to listen to me."

"Gotten my way? Are you crazy?" He clenched his hands into fists. "Nothing in the last eighteen months has been my choice."

"Yes, it has." She bent over, jabbing her index finger into his chest. "Your recovery has been all your way. We've let you be, only stopping by when you let us, trying to make it as easy as possible for you to get back to life—"

"I don't have a life!"

Her mouth dropped open, and she drew back, shaking her head. "You have a life. If you can't see it, there's no hope for you. What happened in here, Sam?" She pointed to her heart, her eyes glistening. "Why won't you let anyone in?"

"I did!" He searched her eyes. Tried to stuff down his emotions and failed. "I let her down. I wanted to be the man she needed, and instead, I put Parker in danger."

"Pshaw." She gave a dismissive wave of her hand. "Parker tripped and fell. He'll have many more falls in his life, with or without you watching him."

"You don't understand." He pinched the bridge of his nose. "I couldn't get to him. He crawled under the Christmas tree. I couldn't reach in and grab him. I couldn't keep him safe."

"Sam, when your cousin Braedon was two, I was helping Joe fix the sink. Braedon was sitting on the couch, watching *Sesame Street*, and I turned my back for a minute. I didn't hear him and got worried. I found him on his bedroom floor, choking on something. I put him over my knees and whacked his back to try to dislodge it. Nothing came out. Fear buzzed through me, and I prayed, frantically begging God to save him. I yelled for Joe, and he raced in there, took one look at Braedon and stuck his finger down his little throat. Braedon threw up, and there in the middle was a quarter. I couldn't keep my baby safe, either. But it didn't stop me from trying."

"It's not the same."

"Sure it is."

"He was your son. Of course you kept trying. What choice did you have?"

"The same one you could have, Sam." She patted his cheek. "I have the feeling Celeste cares for you. And if I'm not mistaken, you feel the same about her and Parker. You're not in control of the universe. God is. Let Him protect your loved ones. Don't let Celeste slip away."

He not only was letting her slip away, he'd been the one to push her out the door.

"God hasn't done a very good job of protecting." The instant it was out of his mouth, shame filled him. And anger—at himself. He was tired of bottling so much anger.

"Still blaming God?" She inclined her head. "If He's not good at protecting, why is Parker on his way home with his mom as we speak? Why are you still here, for that matter? Do you know how close you were to death when the boat hit you?" She sighed. "I'm going to get the car. While I'm gone, you'd best think about the worm chewing a hole in your heart. Slay it soon, or it'll steal the best part of you."

She spun on her heel and marched her tight jeans and purple running shoes down the sidewalk and out of his sight.

Every word she said came back to him, stabbing like ice picks. He blew out a breath, watching it puff in front of his face before disappearing. He shivered under his sweater.

There *was* a worm eating his heart. But he didn't know how to slay it. Ever since meeting Celeste, he'd been able to keep it at bay, but today it had won.

How could he slay what he couldn't define?

Fear.

Fear? Fear of what?

I need her. I'm afraid of needing her. I can survive without walking, but if I give her my heart, if I trust God the way Aunt Sally said, I might not survive another blow. What if God takes her from me?

The fear he lived with now was easier than the fear he'd take on if he committed to Celeste and Parker. The earth would keep spinning if anything happened to him, but his world would collapse into a pile of rubble if he married Celeste and lost her or Parker.

The only way to deal with the worm was to give it a corner to live in.

And to keep those closest to him out.

Chapter Fourteen

Celeste wrapped her hands around a mug of hot cocoa and drew her legs under her body later that evening. After leaving the hospital, she'd driven to the cabin, packed a bag of clothes and headed to her parents' house. Times like this called for the warmth of her childhood home. She stared out the large window next to the couch. Stars blinked beyond the outline of tree branches. An old Christmas movie was on TV. What used to be the most wonderful time of the year had officially become an annual contest for the most devastating events in her life.

And, yes, Sam's rejection was devastating.

Whipped cream melted on top of the cocoa, and she took a sip, barely noticing the sweet liquid. She'd put on her favorite flannel red-and-white pajamas and covered her lap with a fuzzy throw, but neither comforted her the way they should.

She'd been wrestling with her thoughts for hours. Strange she hadn't cried—not once—since he'd dismissed her.

Maybe her tear ducts had dried up. She felt lost. Empty.

Numb.

"Parker fell asleep. It was a treat to tuck him in again." Mom carried her own mug of cocoa into the living room and sat in the recliner. "Aah, feels like old times. I miss you. I miss Parker. I miss us all living together. I'm not going in to work tomorrow, so you just relax here as long as you'd like, and I'll take care of Parker."

Celeste tried to smile.

"I know you'll tell me what's on your mind when you're ready, but will you at least fill me in on what the doctor said?" If the crinkles above her nose didn't reveal her concern, the nervous tapping of her fingernail against the mug did.

"What we thought. No more surgery." Saying those words rubbed her throat raw. She took another drink of her cocoa, but it didn't ease the ache.

Mom set her cup down and shifted to face her. "Tell me everything. Did he give you an explanation? Alternative?"

Who cared? Her face could be a mangled mess and it wouldn't matter, because Sam didn't want her, he'd kicked her out of his life and she had to somehow go on without him.

Celeste lifted a shoulder in a shrug. "He said surgery wouldn't help. I pretty much tuned out after that. Sally called about Parker, and I left."

"That's it?" Mom crossed one leg over the other. "I knew I should have gone with you."

"I'm a big girl. I handled it, Mom."

"Obviously that's not true or you would have listened to what he said. Did he mention laser treatments?"

The warmth of her childhood home suddenly stifled her. Was she twelve again, getting lectured for not listening in class? Didn't she have enough to deal with?

"He handed me a bunch of pamphlets." She absentmindedly waved backward and resumed staring out the window.

"And you didn't look at them?" The way she said it made it sound as if Celeste had thrown away the Hope Diamond.

"Look, Mom, I have bigger problems, okay?" She swung her legs over the side of the couch, tossed the throw off her and marched out of the room. *Great.* Not only was she being treated like a twelve-year-old, she was acting like one, too.

Her mother followed her to the kitchen. "I'm sorry. I know how much this appointment meant to you. Give it a few days and look over the material. We can figure out your options then." She wrapped her arms around Celeste, and Celeste puddled into them, not realizing how much she craved her mother's embrace.

A few minutes later, she stepped back. "I think I'll turn in."

"It's only eight." The worry lines returned to Mom's forehead.

What did it matter? She wouldn't sleep. She had so much to think about.

So much to *avoid* thinking about.

After kissing Mom's cheek, she padded to her old room, shut the door and slid under the covers.

Ironically, hearing she wouldn't be having more surgery was the least of her problems. In fact, for the first time since the accident she really didn't care. What did it matter if her face looked the way it did? Since moving to Lake Endwell, she'd been getting through life okay. She could go to the grocery store now. She'd been to the library. Awkward questions? She had answers. Stares? She was used to them. She was even ready to attend church again.

The scars no longer mattered. She'd be raising Parker alone, anyhow. She couldn't imagine—didn't want to imagine—a life with anyone but Sam. And he'd been shockingly clear he didn't want her in his.

But why?

She didn't think it was her face. He'd been grim before she told him the verdict. Whatever changed him had happened before she told him about the results of her appointment.

So what was it?

She searched her thoughts for any clue. He'd been so sweet this morning, asking if she wanted Parker and him to come with her. And she'd said no, she wanted to go alone.

Was that it? Had he felt rejected by her?

And then the hospital and Parker falling... Maybe he blamed Parker for causing him to fall. Sam had acted strange when Parker reached for him.

She shook her head. That couldn't be it. Sam adored Parker. He not only said it, he acted like it, too.

Which brought her back to her. Sam must have realized she wasn't the right woman for him.

Did he think she'd hurt him?

She would *never* hurt him.

But that might not be the kind of hurt he was talking about. He'd told her he wanted to carry a child on his shoulders. That he wasn't having a family until he could walk on his own. What if the doctor had told him he'd never walk again? Was that why he rejected her?

Acid turned her stomach into a battlefield. She clutched the covers to her neck, squeezing her eyes shut.

She might never know why he changed his mind.

And in the meantime, she'd try to forget the brilliant blue of Sam's eyes, the funny things he said, the way he made her feel at ease, the strength of his arms around her, his kiss…

Stop it! Just stop!

If she could fall asleep for two or three weeks, sleep right through this heartache…

Her brother was dead. Her best friend was dead. And she was the one who had to go on without them. Two giant holes in her life.

Losing Josh had been like losing her childhood.

Losing Brandy had been like losing her twin.

Losing Sam was like losing a lung.

She didn't know how she'd survive without him.

He hated it here.

Sam didn't turn on the Christmas tree lights or any other light, for that matter. The glow of a hockey game from the television was the only brightness in the dark room. His swollen leg throbbed even with it wrapped in ice and propped on the couch. This cottage felt like a prison.

Would he always live like this?

Alone.

Helpless.

Miserable.

And why? It was his fault.

Aunt Sally's lecture kept going around in his head, and every time he tried to shush it, it grew louder. *Still blaming God?*

Yeah. He was. And he was tired of it.

Granddad kept a Bible in the end-table drawer. Sam had never been a big Bible reader. He'd gone to Sunday school for years, attended church his entire life, and it had been enough. But ever since the accident, he'd closed his heart to God. Refused church, prayer and the Bible. Until recently.

The more he tried to shut God out, the deeper his emptiness grew.

He was tired of blaming God.

Sam opened the drawer and strained to reach the Bible. Finally, he grasped it and hauled it on his lap.

For a long time he stared at it. He didn't know where to begin.

Lord, I'm here. I'm desperate. You know that. I can't go on like this. I'm tired of being angry. I'm tired of being afraid. I'm really tired of shutting You out. I don't know if You care anymore. I don't deserve it. I mean, I've blamed You for all my problems.

Maybe he should forget this.

He set the Bible next to him on the couch. He'd pushed God away too long. How could he expect God to forgive him with a snap of the fingers?

Shouldn't he be on his knees, repenting?

Even if he could get on his knees, he didn't have the energy to repent.

Frustration mounted, and he snatched the Bible and opened it. Ecclesiastes. *Everything is meaningless?* Terrific. Not exactly the words he'd been hoping for.

He flipped through, landing on the second book of Corinthians. He skimmed a section about the apostle Paul, stopping short when he read a verse. He double-checked it. Paul had been given a thorn in his flesh, and he begged God to take it from him, but God refused. Why?

Why did God refuse Paul?

Why did You refuse me?

Sam read the rest of the chapter and frowned. God didn't say He refused because He didn't love Paul or because Paul deserved the thorn. The scripture gave a different reason—that God's grace was sufficient and His strength was made perfect in weakness.

God's grace was sufficient? His strength was made perfect in weakness?

It didn't make sense. How could strength be made perfect in weakness?

Because it will force me to rely on God instead of myself.

He didn't want to. He didn't want to put all his trust in God. He wanted some of the power, some way of controlling his destiny—wasn't that natural?

How was that working out for him, though?

Lord, I don't know if I can give it all up to You. I just don't know if I can.

He wanted some say in his life.

Yeah, and he was doing so much with it. He ground his teeth together.

Okay, You win. What do You want me to do? What is Your will?

He waited, hoping for an answer to hit him upside the head. It didn't.

His phone vibrated. He checked the text. Bryan wanted to know if he should pick Sam up for tomorrow's meeting at Tommy's dealership.

The doctor hadn't told him he couldn't return to work. He'd told him to take it slow, use the wheelchair. But could he?

Maybe it was time to pay *his* dealership a visit. He texted Bryan back.

Celeste slept until noon, shocked she'd gotten to sleep at all. When was the last time she'd slept in? Before the accident, that was for sure. She changed into a pair of worn jeans and a soft oversize black sweater, then padded into the kitchen to see how Mom and Parker fared. The kitchen was empty except for a note on the counter from her mom saying she was taking Parker out for an adventure and they'd be back later that afternoon.

After fixing a bowl of cereal, Celeste sat at the dining table and tried to keep her mind blank. Impossible.

What was Sam doing now? Did he miss her? Did he regret pushing her away?

Tomorrow was the parade. Sally had told her all about the food vendors and festivities they'd lined up at City Park. It had sounded like so much fun. Mostly because she'd be with Sam. Just the two of them.

And now there was no two of them. No clutching take-out coffee as Shriners drove down the street in miniature cars and the marching band played. No distraction from her memories, from the anniversary of the accident.

Dread filled her at the thought of getting through tomorrow. She'd missed Brandy's funeral because she'd still been in the hospital. Maybe that was part of the reason she felt so low.

She'd never said goodbye to Brandy.

The distraction of the parade had been a lifeline so she wouldn't have to face tomorrow and what was taken from her.

How could she distract herself now?

What if she didn't distract herself? What if she faced the anniversary head-on?

Today.

Right now.

Celeste set the empty bowl in the sink and slipped her feet into boots. As much as she didn't want to, her inner being shouted she needed this. She needed to go back to the accident site and face the doubts and fears swirling in her gut. Get some closure. If closure was possible.

Fifteen minutes later she parked her minivan on the side of the road. It really was a barren stretch of blacktop. No houses nearby. A field with a fresh buzz cut from the fall crop harvest—corn from the looks of it— stood in washed-out gold shades to her right. The telephone pole her car hit last year rose tall and menacing against the colorless sky. The ditch was deep and full of overgrown yellow grass and weeds. The opposite side of the road held the same view.

Celeste stepped outside, burrowing deep into her winter coat. Hands in her pockets, she stood next to the ditch. Cold wind blew her hair around her neck and bit at her face. She barely noticed. Just stared at the pole.

An ordinary thing. A tall piece of wood. Once a tree.

It had taken Brandy from her.

It had taken more.

So much more.

Something drew her to that telephone pole. She couldn't name it. She needed to cross over and touch it.

Taking a few steps back, she ran and leaped across the ditch, falling to one knee as she landed. She rose, brushing off her jeans, and trudged to the pole. Craned her neck back. A pair of birds perched on the wire. And the pole grew taller, reaching higher than before.

"I hate you," she whispered, wishing she had a chain saw or an ax. Anything to chop it down.

The words opened a cavity she'd hidden inside, and without warning, a flock of thoughts, feelings and impressions flew out.

"You were set in the ground right here." She didn't care she was shouting at an inanimate object. "Not five feet over there. Here. And if you had been there—" she pointed "—my car wouldn't have hit you. We probably would have walked away shaken up with a few scrapes. But that's not what happened. All because of you."

"I hate you," she yelled, kicking at the clump of weeds surrounding it. "I hate you!"

A gust of wind stung her cheeks.

She'd never be able to tell Brandy how much she loved her. How much she meant to her.

"Give her back!" She dropped to her knees. "I want her back."

With her hands covering her face, she wept. Shoulders shaking, the smell of earth in her nose—she didn't try to control her cries. Minutes ticked by as she released every drop of sorrow.

When she had nothing left, she dropped back and sat on the ground.

"I'm sorry, Brandy. I'm so sorry. I should have paid attention. I shouldn't have sung so loudly. I shouldn't have made you come with me. I should have…"

What? What could she possibly have done differently?

It was an accident.

An accident. She hadn't been texting or drinking or driving like a maniac. She'd been going the speed limit.

There was nothing she could have done differently.

It seemed so senseless.

Why? Why had it happened? Why?

She wiped her nose and gazed up at the telephone pole.

And it was as if a lightning bolt went through her chest.

He knows. He knows how I feel. He knows why. And He doesn't want me to feel it anymore.

Jesus had been nailed to a cross. A piece of wood.

Planted in the ground. Similar to this pole that took Brandy.

Both had been taken by trees.

He gave His life for me. He died on the cross for me. God knows how broken I feel, because He lost His Son.

"You get it, don't You, God?" Celeste scooted to the pole, sitting at its base with her back to it. "You lost the One most important to You, too. You understand. You know how I feel. I don't know why I didn't realize it until now."

A wave of peace crested over her body.

God had given His Son to save her, to save Brandy and Josh and everyone else who believed. He knew what it was like to grieve.

The pole at her back wasn't the enemy.

I need to let go. I've been blaming myself for the accident, but that's what it was—an accident. I will probably never know why it happened, but I can go on. God, help me let go.

She shifted, pressing her cheek against the smooth, cold wood. Just a telephone pole. A tree at one time.

For the first time in a year, she felt inner peace. Not on edge. She wasn't holding back a hundred anxieties.

She felt open.

Free.

And she let herself remember all the things that had been too hard to reflect on all year. The precious memories she'd never let go. Two little girls meant to be best friends. Jumping rope at recess, riding bikes all summer long, singing to the radio, watching movies, the countless sleepovers. Giggling, gossiping, crying, just being together. Holding Brandy's bouquet on her wedding day.

Holding her hand at Josh's funeral. And laughing and singing with her the night she died.

Celeste sat there until the cold seeped through her clothes and she couldn't control her shivers.

Brandy and Josh were in heaven. Not coming back. She would see them again, eventually. She had no choice but to go on without them in her life.

But she had a choice about Sam. And whether he wanted her in his life or not, she needed to tell him how much he meant to her. She didn't want to regret *not* telling him.

How could she convince him there were no guarantees? That getting hurt could happen. That random events shattered lives sometimes, and no one knew why.

Wasn't the thought of a forever love worth the risk?

It was worth it to her. She was going to try.

Friday night at eight, Sam stared at the dark glass entryway of his dealership. Could he find the answers he was looking for here? The employees had all gone home for the night. Bryan typed in the alarm code and opened the door so Sam could wheel inside. As Sam waited, Bryan flicked the lights on. Several impressions slammed into his mind.

Pride. This was the building and business he was responsible for. He'd built it. He'd planned it. And it was still here, waiting for him.

Relief. His brothers and employees were taking good care of it. Not a speck of dirt or a desk out of place.

Memories. Strolling through it the day before the grand opening. Confident, excited and nervous. On his two strong legs. On both feet.

He blew out a breath.

"It looks exactly the same." He rolled through the

showroom, slowly moving past the shiny cars displayed inside. "Well, the vehicles are different. I like this one. Who chose it?"

"I did." Bryan slipped the keys in his pocket and stayed close to Sam. "Did the doctor say you could still come back to work?"

"I can come back." He didn't add that he'd been able to come back for months—in a wheelchair.

"Good. You still want to?"

"I've always wanted to." *Just not like this.* "I'm going to check out my office."

Bryan studied him a minute, most likely seeing way more than Sam wanted him to. "I'll wait here. Holler if you need me."

He didn't linger. Spinning forward, he passed the customer waiting room and a row of cubicles for the sales staff. He rolled down a hallway. Faced a door with a shiny nameplate. *Sam Sheffield.*

His office.

In another life.

He jiggled the handle, but it was locked. He'd forgotten his keys. "Hey, Bryan, do you have the key to my office?"

Bryan's footsteps grew louder. "What do you need?"

"The key." He pointed to the handle. "Do you have it?"

"I have them all." Bryan grinned, pulling out a ring full of keys. After unlocking it, he returned to the showroom while Sam moved through the doorway.

Framed degrees and certificates hung on the walls the way he remembered. A picture of him cutting the ribbon at the grand opening sat on the desk. A smiling photo of the Sheffields taken a few Christmases ago was centered between bookshelves. His office smelled like new carpet and stale air.

The leather chair behind the mahogany desk reminded him of poring over reports, signing checks, making deals.

He wanted to sit in it again.

After setting the brake on the wheelchair, he pushed himself up to a standing position and let his left leg bear his weight. Using the desktop to keep his balance, he circled around and sat in the chair.

It felt the same.

Felt like success.

His lips lifted into the briefest smile. Then the reality of his situation choked it away. Emotions churned, but he didn't want them. Couldn't deal with them on top of everything else. He opened the top desk drawer. A slim stack of papers greeted him.

He took them out and scanned the first sheet. Dated the day before his accident. A request from a local youth volleyball team to sponsor their season. *Sorry, ladies. Missed responding to that one.* Setting it aside, he read the next. His handwriting. Notes about a possible dealership location forty-five minutes away. A wrinkled map with highlights. He'd forgotten he'd driven out to it a few days before his life changed permanently.

He kept his eyes fixed on the wall, but he didn't see anything. The plans he'd had trickled back. The Realtor taking him to a possible site for the next phase of his business plan. Scanning the area, mentally building on the field. Shielding his eyes, trying to figure out if the two-lane road would help or hurt traffic flow.

Sam put the papers back in the drawer and shut it. Propping his elbows on the desk, he let his forehead fall into his hands.

I don't know if I can do this. I'm not the same man.

The past eighteen months—in the hospital, the physical rehab center, the cottage—flashed before him. Alone. Bored. In pain.

This dealership, this office was his. If he wanted it.

Next to the desk, the wheelchair mocked him. And the urge to yell, to beat his fists, to protest his situation consumed him.

His jaw clenched. He was so tired of clinging to this anger, this rage.

What would it take for him to let it go?

Words pressed against his heart.

No. I can't. Not those words.

If he let them out, they would either release him or destroy him. He wasn't sure which. He'd been avoiding them for months, afraid of their power.

But he had no fight left.

Only surrender.

Fear congealed in his throat. The dreaded words formed in his head.

I'm sorry, God. For blaming You. For expecting You to do whatever I wanted. For telling You the terms. I need You. I can't do this on my own anymore.

The dam inside him broke, and he couldn't control it. His eyes ached as tears spilled out, and his shoulders shook as he began to cry. For the man he used to be. For the man he was now. For the lost months, the pain, the dreams he'd clung to, the ones he'd given up on.

When he'd emptied everything out, he straightened, wiping his face with his sleeve.

Bryan stood in the doorway. Compassion glowed from his pale blue eyes. Three strides and he was at Sam's side. Bryan set his hand on Sam's shoulder and bent to hug him.

"I'm sorry. I hate that this happened to you."

Sam cleared his throat, shaking his head.

"You're not ready." Bryan rounded the desk and sat in one of the chairs facing Sam. "I'll run it. Don't worry. It will be here. Take your time."

Peace settled over Sam's soul.

The accident took full use of my legs, but it didn't take all of me.

Strangely, he felt stronger than he had in months.

He could handle this. He could do it.

"This is mine." Sam spread his palms over the desk. "I'm coming back."

"You're not ready."

"I *am* ready. I could have come back months ago, but I didn't want to work in a wheelchair. I still don't want to, but you know what? I'm going to. Who cares if I can't walk? I can still run this place."

"Are you sure?" Bryan looked like he was chewing on a tough strip of beef jerky. "You don't have to."

"Yes, I do. If I don't, I might never come back. I need this. Need my job. Need something to occupy my time."

And he needed Celeste. And Parker.

He needed them more than he needed the dealership.

They were the best part of him. And he'd thrown them out.

"Bry?"

Bryan raised his eyebrows.

"I probably won't ever walk without a cane or a limp. I might always need this wheelchair to some extent."

"Yeah, so?"

Heat climbed his neck. He loosened his collar. "Can a guy like me, with my limitations, be a good husband? A good father?"

Bryan's face contorted in confusion. "Why wouldn't you be?"

He didn't want to explain. He shouldn't have brought it up.

"You don't need to walk to love someone." Now it was Bryan's turn to look embarrassed. "To cherish them."

"And when a baby cries in the night? I might not be able to get it out of the crib."

"Your wife would."

"What if she's sick?"

Bryan rubbed his chin and stared into space. "You can always call one of us. Or you could hire a nanny at night. There might be special cribs you could buy."

True. But maybe Bryan was missing the point.

"Okay, but when all the dads are lifting a toddler on their shoulders and my kid wants to sit on mine, what am I going to do? I'll let him down."

"Buy him a balloon or something. He'll get over it."

True again. But was Bryan still missing the point?

Bryan leaned back, crossing his arms. "I think you're scared. I know scared. The worst scare of my life—the thought of losing you—prompted me to get over my biggest fear. You helped me give my heart to Jade. The night of your accident, I left your hospital room and felt destroyed. And she came to me like a gift from God."

"I didn't know that."

"If you're afraid of taking a chance on Celeste—and don't deny it, we all know you like her—don't be. I had a lot of excuses why it wouldn't work between Jade and me, too. But that was fear feeding me a bunch of lies." Bryan leaned forward. "Tommy told me something when I was being a thickheaded dolt about Jade. He asked, 'Do you believe you're divinely guided?' You'll have to ask yourself the same thing."

"I shut God out for a long time."

"He was still there. He's always there." Bryan flourished his hand. "When you trust God, He will always lead you to the right turn in the road."

The right turn in the road.

"You're right." Sam could see it all—God's hand in his life. The accident had happened, but God had allowed him to live. God had saved him, saved his leg, protected him and sent Celeste when he needed her most. "So I should fight for Celeste and Parker?"

"I wouldn't let anything keep me from Jade." Bryan grinned. "Does Celeste feel the same?"

Sam blew out a breath and shrugged. "I was a jerk yesterday. I honestly don't know. Wouldn't blame her if she hated me."

"Get ready to grovel." Bryan laughed.

"Real funny." Even if Sam groveled, could he convince Celeste they were right for each other?

Maybe.

If he did it right…

Chapter Fifteen

Celeste had to tell Sam she loved him. Today.

Or tomorrow.

No, today.

Down by the lake on Saturday morning, she wrapped her arms around herself as the sun rose. Mom and Dad had agreed to watch Parker the rest of the weekend, so she'd driven back to the cabin late last night to strategize. To plan. To pretend she wasn't taking the biggest risk of her life.

She needed to gather her courage and march up to Sam's door.

She wasn't ready yet.

The sun's glow lit the sky above the tree line behind the lake. Darkness faded little by little. One year ago, she'd put in eight hours at the most boring job in the world, gone back to her apartment, thrown on her cutest outfit and driven straight to Brandy's.

Today could end up as traumatic as a year ago, or it could be the best day ever.

Either way, she had a feeling she'd be okay.

God was with her. Guiding her. Supporting her.

She was ready for this.

She reviewed her plan. Since she'd slept all of forty-seven minutes last night, she'd had plenty of time to get ready. She wore her favorite jeans, warm boots and a red sweater. She'd straightened her already straight hair.

Her makeup was light. It didn't cover her scars, and she didn't want it to. Either she was good enough for Sam with her scars or she wasn't. And if she wasn't, well, he wasn't right for her, either.

Stop procrastinating. Go over there, already.

Celeste headed back up the lawn. When she reached the driveway between her cabin and Sam's cottage, she stopped short. On her porch steps, Sam leaned against his crutches. Their gazes locked. She couldn't move. Couldn't think.

What was he doing there? Out of his wheelchair? On her steps?

"Hey," he said, extending his neck in greeting.

"Hey." *Brilliant response.*

"We need to talk." The words brought mixed feelings—hope, yes, but fear and disappointment over their last encounter, too.

"Now?" She hated that her head and heart were clashing right now. Her plan to tell him she loved him fled out the back door, and all that was left was uncertainty. "What if I don't want to?"

He hung his head. "Look, I'm sorry. And I don't blame you, but we need to talk."

She nodded, wishing his apology could wipe away all their problems, but it couldn't. They *did* need to talk. She could invite him in, but she wanted all her memories in the cabin to be good. If he was going to break her heart, she preferred he do it somewhere else. "Not here."

"Let's go to town, then."

"I'll get my keys." Celeste went inside and grabbed

her purse, refusing to get her hopes up. He could have any number of things to say. Maybe he wanted her to move out. Since he didn't need her to drive him around, he didn't want her living there. Could that be it?

He would never be that cruel.

They drove in silence until Sam told her to park in a lot behind the most picture-perfect church she'd ever seen. Huge wreaths with big red bows hung from the double doors, and holly bushes were planted around the front porch.

"Here we are." He waited for her to bring his wheel-chair around and then wheeled himself to a bench in front of the church. "Looks like it's getting ready to snow again."

As if on cue, snowflakes started falling. He sat on the bench and held his hand out. "Come here."

She obeyed, shivering at the cold seeping under her jeans. This wasn't how she'd planned it. She was supposed to go to him, tell him what was in her heart—when she was ready.

She was not ready.

"I'm sorry, Celeste."

The block party raging in her veins lowered a notch. Another apology wasn't what she wanted. She wanted a declaration.

"No, I mean it. I was stupid. I hurt your feelings, and I'm sorry."

"Apology accepted." Why did her voice sound as if it was six miles away? Because his feelings didn't match hers.

He wiped a finger across his eyebrow. Seemed nervous.

Well, join the club, buddy.

"Celeste, I was in a bad place when we met." He

faced her. "Bitter. Angry. Sorry for myself. You changed all that."

She did?

"I saw how you rebounded from your accident. Raising Parker. Starting over in a new town. I admired that. And you gave me the courage to start living again. And I mean, really living. Like leaving the cottage and thinking about work. I even went back to church. This is my church, by the way."

Her throat felt fuzzy. Thoughts jammed in her mind, but she couldn't make sense of them. "It's really pretty."

He nodded. "It is. But that's not important. The more progress I made with my leg, the more hope I felt. Until Thursday. Everything kind of fell apart on Thursday. It wasn't your fault. It was mine. My breakdown had been brewing for a long time."

She winced. Usually when a woman heard the words *it's not your fault, it's mine*, it meant a guy was blowing her off. Was Sam here to blow her off? Or wait—hadn't he already done that?

"I blamed God for not healing me. I let my pride get in the way of going back to work. I pushed away my family and friends. And then you came along."

She met his eyes then—those stunning blue eyes— and a glimmer of hope lit in her chest. He looked at her with such intensity, such need.

"I tried to push you out of my life because I was scared. I thought you needed a man who could protect you, take care of you and help you. I'm not going to pretend I'm that man. I can't carry a baby around on these legs. This week, I couldn't even keep Parker safe for more than an hour. Watching him fall and hit his head because I couldn't pick him up just about broke me, Celeste. I love him."

"I know you do." She did know. What she didn't know was how he felt about her. "You lost a lot in your accident. You had every right to be angry, Sam."

"I shouldn't have blamed God."

"Well, I blamed myself for Brandy dying. I told myself I'd been driving too fast, enjoying our night out too much. Yesterday I even blamed the telephone pole. I wanted it to make sense, but I'll never know why it happened. I had to accept it. Finally, I do. Do you still blame God?"

He shook his head. "No. Like you, I may never understand why I went through this, but God knows why. He loves me and that has to be good enough."

"I'm glad you got right with Him."

"Me, too."

The words she'd been getting up the nerve to say sat on the tip of her tongue.

"Celeste, I need to get right with you, too." He took her hands in his. "I think you're the most beautiful woman I've ever seen. I'm sorry your appointment didn't go the way you hoped, but I've never noticed your scars. I see your big brown eyes and your long, shiny hair. You have a slightly crooked tooth that drives me wild. I see your heart. The way you love Parker with a love so big it can't be contained. I see more than you know, and I love it. I love everything I see. Everything about you. I love you."

He loved her?

But what about his words at the hospital? She had to know for sure if he really meant what he was saying. "At the hospital you said my scars mattered."

His eyes darkened. "Not the way you think. I was afraid of letting you down. I know you'd been let down by the accident and then by not hearing what you wanted from the doctor. Your scars only mattered because I convinced myself I would be one more letdown in your life."

"You could never let me down."

"I could, Celeste. And I probably will."

Sam watched Celeste's expression as his words sank in. Her throat moved as she swallowed, and her hair slipped over her face. He wanted to run his fingers through the silky strands. But he wasn't selling himself as anything more than what he was. If they were going to have a future together, he had to lay out exactly what life with him would be like.

What if he did and she rejected him?

At least he wouldn't have any regrets.

He caressed the back of her hand with his thumb. "Ever since you walked through my door in October, I've been trying to convince myself that this—" he gestured to his right leg "—isn't forever. That I could make it better. Be who I wanted to be. And I wanted to be a man who could carry a bride over the threshold, who could hold a baby during late-night feedings, who wouldn't limp but would be on both feet protecting his loved ones."

Her face, pink from the cold air, oozed sympathy. She squeezed his hand.

"You've had a hard life," he said. "I don't want to make it harder. I'm being selfish."

"You make it easier," she blurted. "I don't need a guy to carry me over the threshold or carry a baby or any of that. I need someone who loves me, scars and all. Someone who will be my partner and love Parker like he's his own son."

"What if you change your mind five years from now?" he asked.

"I've learned we have no guarantees. I might not be

here five years from now. You might not be. But I don't want to go through those years without my best friend."

He scratched his chin. "But Brandy's gone."

She laughed. "I'm talking about you. You're my best friend. You're my safe place. I tell you everything, and I love you, Sam. I love you, too."

His heartbeat pounded, and his chest felt ready to burst. Could it be this easy? When everything else for the past eighteen months had been so hard?

Who cared? He was taking it. Grabbing it.

Sam wrapped his arms around her and drew her to him. Her lips were close, and he kissed her. Drank in their softness. Tasted a hint of coffee and vanilla. Was filled with the sensation of rightness, of his future, of forever.

Before he got carried away, he owed it to both of them to say everything on his mind. He ended the kiss and brushed her cheek with his lips.

"I may always need the wheelchair, Celeste. I'll probably always have a limp. I've lived with chronic pain every day since my accident. It might never go away. I can't carry groceries indoors or play volleyball with you at a picnic. I can't even drive anywhere, although I hope that will change soon. Are you sure you can accept that?"

She cupped his face with her hands. A smile full of joy lit her face. "I'll bring the groceries in, and you can help put them away. I hate volleyball. I like driving. And you're acting like you bring nothing to a relationship. You support me. You brought me out of my shell. You allowed me to run again. You make Parker laugh. You're so good with him."

"I'm worried about watching him. Worried he'll get hurt, and it will be my fault."

"Don't worry. You're great with him. He's going to get hurt sometimes. That's how life is."

He nodded.

"I think he's been trying to call you Daddy. If you want me to stop him, I will…" Worry dimmed her eyes.

"I don't want him to stop. I don't want any of this to stop. I feel like I'm in a dream—a good dream, finally. I don't want to wake up."

"It had better not be a dream. If it is, it's the best one I've ever had."

He leaned in, kissing her again. She twined her arm around him, sinking her fingers in the hair at his nape. Her gentle touch undid him, made him forget why he had ever doubted they should be together. He kissed her slowly, savoring this woman who'd saved him from the pit he'd sunk into.

Thank You, God. Thank You for sending her here, for giving us both another chance at life. For leading us to each other.

Celeste broke free with a shy smile. They stared at each other for a long moment.

"Are you still up for the parade?" He pushed her soft hair away from her face.

"Are you?" Her nose scrunched in concern.

"I am. The doc told me I have to protect my leg at all costs, though, so I'm stuck in the wheelchair today."

A smile bigger than Lake Endwell spread across her face. "Fine with me. Besides, you promised."

"I did. And it's officially a date." He grinned. "Let's get breakfast, then head up to Main Street. I know just the spot on the parade route."

Celeste smoothed her skirt over her knees and peeked back at the church entrance for the twelfth time in two minutes. Why was she so nervous? Parker would be a great baby Jesus.

"Are you as nervous as I am?" Sam squeezed her arm.

"More." They sat in the second row of Brandy's church Christmas Eve night. The children's service would be starting soon. Celeste, Sam and Parker had stopped by her parents' house earlier, and the introductions had gone better than she could have hoped for. When they got to the church, Parker happily went to Shelby.

The days since the parade had flown by in a blur of shopping, wrapping gifts and watching Christmas movies—all with Sam, of course. The parade had been wonderful. She and Sam had sipped coffee and joined his siblings and their families on the sidewalk of Main Street. The marching band played "Deck the Halls" as dancers spun and leaped down the street. Miss Lake Endwell had waved from the back of a silver convertible, and Shriners drove miniature cars. The best part? Sam had held her hand the entire parade.

As he'd held it every day since.

"Here comes Grandma Pearl." She sucked in a breath and exchanged a charged look with Sam. "I hope Parker does okay."

They rose to let Grandma Pearl sit with them, and after she settled in, she turned to Celeste. "It was so nice of you to join me for the service. I know you have your own church to go to. Where's Parker?"

Celeste had talked to Sue Roper earlier, and they'd agreed not to say anything. To let Grandma Pearl realize that Parker was baby Jesus on her own. After the service they would reveal why they wanted to surprise her.

"You'll see."

A hymn began to play and the congregation stood. Dressed up in costumes, the excited children strode to the front of the church, stopping where they'd been directed. Shelby, dressed as Mary, held Parker—who was wrapped in a beige cloth—as she walked to the manger set. Matt, dressed as Joseph, stood beside her, a staff in his hand.

Grandma Pearl pressed her hand against her chest. "Oh!"

"Are you okay?" Celeste asked.

"Parker," she said breathlessly. "He's baby Jesus!" Her eyes glistened with tears and she searched Celeste's face. Celeste nodded, grinning at the wonder in her expression. Grandma Pearl dug through her enormous black purse and found a handkerchief, wiping her eyes. When she pulled herself together, she took Celeste's hand in both of hers and held tightly. "I never thought I'd see the day… You've made me so happy."

The service continued with recitations and hymns. Parker sat quietly in the fake manger, and Shelby kept a hand on him, brushing the hair from his forehead. The moment came for the shepherds to arrive. One of the sheep ran crying down the aisle to his mother. The movement startled Parker, and he sat up, spotting Celeste and Sam.

"Mama! Dada!" He held his arms out. Muffled laughter spread throughout the church. Celeste covered her mouth and glanced at Sam. He grinned, winking at her. Shelby soothed Parker, and he quieted down. The rest of the service flew by in a blur, and before they knew it, they were in the fellowship hall with Sue Roper, a swarm of parents and hyper kids.

As Sue and several women explained their surprise

to Grandma Pearl, Celeste noticed Sam approaching her dad. Dad clapped him on the shoulder and nodded.

Hmm...

Sam returned to her. "Your parents are taking Parker home for the night. I have a surprise for you."

"What kind of surprise?" This was getting strange.

"It's an early Christmas present."

"Are you sure about this?"

"Never been so sure about anything in my life."

Thirty minutes later, Celeste sat on Sam's couch, wondering what on earth she was doing there. Sam had disappeared to his bedroom. He'd refused to say anything about the surprise on the ride over. Instead, he talked about the presents he'd bought his sisters and the Christmas movie he'd watched late last night. Stalling and evading. She had to admit he was good at it. The lights from the tree they'd decorated together sparkled, casting a Christmas glow.

And then there he was.

She stopped breathing.

Absolutely gorgeous.

His blue eyes radiated love. A dark gray sweater perfectly showcased his broad shoulders. Dress pants hid the brace she could just make out beneath the fabric. Something was in his hand in addition to his crutches. He approached, carefully lowering himself to the couch next to her.

"I didn't know where or how to do this, but when I think of you, I know God sent you here to me. You helped me get right with Him again. So this, where we met, is perfect."

"For what?" Nervous anticipation made her words rush out, but she wasn't scared.

"This cottage is where you helped set me free." He looked serious. "Give me your hands."

She held out her hands. He massaged them with his. The intensity in his eyes made her gulp.

"Celeste, I love you. We both know life can change in an instant. That's why I'm doing this now. I already spoke with your dad." He held a small black box. "You're the only woman for me. I love you. I love Parker. I want to be your husband. I want to be his daddy. I want forever with you. Will you marry me?"

"Yes, oh, Sam, yes! I love you. I want to be your wife. I want you to be Parker's daddy. And, God willing, we'll have more babies, too, if that's okay with you."

He slid a ring on her finger. A dazzling diamond winked at her.

"I definitely want more babies." His husky tone matched the gleam in his eyes. And he kissed her, thoroughly. "Thank you. Thank you for saying yes."

"Thank you for being my yes."

He kissed her temple. "You'll always be my yes."

Epilogue

Ten months later, Sam stood gripping his cane at the front of the church. He closed his eyes and took a deep breath. Today was the day. He'd met Celeste exactly one year ago, and now she would finally be his wife. *Thank You, Lord.*

"Are you ready?" Bryan, his best man, whispered, nudging him.

"I'm ready." Sam adjusted his tux. The doors were opened and the bridesmaids—his sisters and sisters-in-law—slowly walked up the aisle in matching red dresses. Macy followed, spreading flowers from her basket. Emily, wearing a white dress, and Parker, in a tiny tuxedo, held hands as they ran top speed up the aisle. Laughter erupted from the pews. And then Celeste appeared on her dad's arm.

Breathtaking.

If his knee hadn't been in the brace, it probably would have collapsed at the beauty coming toward him. Her white satin dress had short sleeves, lace and beading. He barely noticed it. It was the woman behind the veil that held him captive. Moments later her dad lifted the veil, put Celeste's hand in Sam's, and together they walked the few steps to the front.

"You're beautiful," he whispered. "I don't have words. You're the most stunning woman I've ever seen."

"I'll never get tired of hearing it," she whispered back.

The pastor opened the Bible. They listened to the scripture. Exchanged vows and rings.

"I now pronounce you man and wife."

He grinned, and she grinned back. When they'd walked all the way back to the entryway where everyone would greet them, Sam propped his cane against the wall, cupped her face in his hands and kissed her.

"Oh, my!" She looked dazed. She rested her palm against his chest. "Just think—one year ago was the day we met. I never would have imagined then that we'd be married now."

"I couldn't walk."

"And my scars were much worse."

"They were never bad." He touched her cheek. Celeste had tried a laser treatment, which had reduced the appearance of her scars. Only two were visible. Not that she could ever be less than exquisitely beautiful in his eyes, but he was glad she'd gotten the results she'd hoped for.

"A lot has changed since then." He kept her close to him as the bridal party approached.

Sam had gone back to work in January—and he was thriving. He no longer had to use his wheelchair at the dealership, but he still needed crutches sometimes. Mostly, he relied on the cane. He was fine with that. And Celeste had been taking online classes to become a teacher. It would be another year until she'd meet the requirements, but in the meantime, the high school cross-country coach had asked her to be an assistant coach.

After the obligatory hug-fest in the receiving line, where Celeste and her mom hugged for so long they had to be broken up and Aunt Sally jumped back in line three times, Sam tapped Bryan's shoulder. "Can we escape?"

"Absolutely." Bryan and Tommy rounded up the bridal party, including Claire and Reed's baby, Robert, for pictures. Then they headed to the reception at Uncle Joe's Restaurant.

Sam didn't smash cake in Celeste's face, but he could tell how tempted she was to smear cake in his. Thankfully, she refrained. The night wore on, and when they'd talked to everyone, Sam pulled Celeste to him, kissed her and said, "It's time."

Her eyes sparkled as she nodded.

"Goodbye, Parker! Have fun with Grandma and Grandpa!" Celeste kissed Parker's cheek one more time and waved as her mom and dad carried him away.

"'Bye, Mama! 'Bye, Dada!" He blew them kisses.

Sam blew them right back. He'd miss the little guy while they were on their honeymoon in Hawaii. Sam leaned on his cane and kept his other hand wrapped around Celeste's waist. He leaned close to her ear. "Let's get out of here. I have a surprise for you."

She twined her arms around his neck. "Last time you said that, we got engaged."

"I know." He tugged her close and kissed her.

"Whew." She fanned herself. "Is it hot in here?"

"Yes. Way too hot. Let's go." He moved toward the door. "I'm not going to convince you to let me drive, am I?" Earlier in the summer, he'd finally been cleared to drive. The freedom meant more to him than words could express.

"No way—I'm driving." She tapped her chin. "I told you I've always wondered what it would be like to drive a truck in a wedding gown."

He laughed. "I think you should wear it every day. You're beautiful in it. Well, you're always beautiful."

They headed out into the cold October air and shivered in Sam's truck as Celeste let it warm up a minute. "So where are we going?"

"The cottage."

"Really? I thought you'd want to go to a hotel or something."

"Nope. I have something I need to do."

"I'll take your word for it."

It didn't take long to get there.

"Wait right there a minute and meet me at the patio door." He raised a finger and got out of the truck, carefully walking up the ramp with his cane. He switched on the little white Christmas lights strung across the porch rail. Then he brought out the wheelchair and turned it so the back would be facing her.

He'd been imagining this moment for months.

A minute later, she ran up the ramp to him, holding her pretty wedding gown in her hands. As soon as she saw the wheelchair, she burst out laughing. It had white balloons attached to the handles and a Just Married sign stuck to the back.

"I've always wanted to carry a bride over the threshold." He sat in the chair and patted his lap. "Hop on. I'm carrying you over."

"I'll hurt your leg." She tentatively stepped in front of him.

"No, you won't." He pulled her down onto his lap. Her full white satin skirt trailed over the edge, and she wrapped her arms around his neck. He held her tightly. He'd never let her go.

"Are you ready?" he asked.

"I'm ready."

And he rolled the chair through the patio and into the cottage.

"Now it's official. Welcome home, Mrs. Sheffield."

* * * * *

If you enjoyed Sam and Celeste's story,
pick up Jill Kemerer's books
about the other Sheffield siblings:

SMALL-TOWN BACHELOR
UNEXPECTED FAMILY
HER SMALL-TOWN ROMANCE

Available now from Love Inspired!

Find more great reads at www.LoveInspired.com

Dear Reader,

When I started writing the Lake Endwell series, Sam Sheffield was a charming guy who embraced a challenge and loved his family. But a boating accident in *Her Small-Town Romance* changed him. His near-death experience and ongoing physical pain and disabilities robbed him of his joy and hope. Spending time with Celeste and Parker showed him he can have a full life again, one with the blessings of a wife and family. Best of all, he finally came to terms with the fact that God loves him and has been with him all this time.

I don't know if I would be as resilient as Sam or Celeste after what they'd been through in their accidents, but I hope I would cling to my faith. God will see us through our hard times. He loves us with a love so big it can't be contained. No matter what problems we face, we have a God who cares. This Christmas season, I encourage you to reflect on one of my favorite Bible passages, Philippians 4:7 (NIV) "And the peace of God, which transcends all understanding, will guard your hearts and your minds in Christ Jesus."

I love connecting with readers. Please stop by my website, www.jillkemerer.com, and email me at jill@jillkemerer.com.

God bless you!
Jill Kemerer

COMING NEXT MONTH FROM
Love Inspired®

Available December 20, 2016

THE COWBOY'S TEXAS FAMILY
Lone Star Cowboy League: Boys Ranch
by Margaret Daley
Rancher Nick McGarrett never wanted a wife and kids—he's content volunteering with the troubled youths at the Triple C Ranch. That is, until Darcy Hill arrives and takes a special interest in an orphaned boy. Can he overcome his reservations to create a future with them?

AN AMISH REUNION
Amish Hearts • by Jo Ann Brown
Hannah Lambright is shocked to learn she has a baby sister. With no experience raising children, she turns to past love Daniel Stoltzfus for aid. As they grow close, Hannah realizes that if she can trust Daniel not to break her heart again, she may finally get her wish: having a family.

HER GUARDIAN RANCHER
Martin's Crossing • by Brenda Minton
Cowboy Daron McKay promised his dying friend to watch over his wife and his child—but he never imagined he'd fall for the beautiful Emma Shaw. As they work to get daughter Jamie through a difficult surgery, can he convince Emma to accept love a second time around?

APPLE ORCHARD BRIDE
Goose Harbor • by Jessica Keller
When he's given custody of his cousin's child, Toby Holcomb moves back to his hometown to start anew as a dad. Working side by side with Jenna Crest on her father's orchard, Toby begins to realize that his life's happiness may depend on a friend from his past.

SECOND CHANCE FATHER
Willow's Haven • by Renee Andrews
Finding out that Jack Simon is the key to breaking through little Cody's barriers, social worker Elise Ramsey refuses to let the reclusive widower hide from the world. Still healing from the loss of his family, can Jack embrace Elise and Cody as his second chance at happily-ever-after?

ROCKY MOUNTAIN COWBOY
by Tina Radcliffe
Joe Gallagher is surprised to find the woman who abandoned him is back in Paradise, Colorado, to be his physical therapist. Single mom Rebecca Simpson knows she hurt the handsome cowboy all those years ago, but if she can earn his trust this could be their chance at forever.

LOOK FOR THESE AND OTHER LOVE INSPIRED BOOKS WHEREVER BOOKS ARE SOLD, INCLUDING MOST BOOKSTORES, SUPERMARKETS, DISCOUNT STORES AND DRUGSTORES.

LICNM1216

A promise to watch out for his late army buddy's little brother might have this single rancher in over his head. But he's not the only one who wants to care for the boy...

Read on for a sneak preview of the fourth book in the **LONE STAR COWBOY LEAGUE: BOYS RANCH** miniseries, *THE COWBOY'S TEXAS FAMILY* by **Margaret Daley**.

As Nick settled behind the steering wheel and started his truck, he slanted a look at Darcy. "So what do you think about the boys ranch?"

"Corey is much better off here than with his dad. He's not happy right now, but then he wasn't happy at home."

"He's scared." That was why Bea had brought him to the barn first to see Nick. "He'll feel better after he meets some of the other boys his age."

"What if he doesn't?" Darcy asked.

"He's confused. He wants to be with his dad, and yet not if he's always being left alone. He doesn't know what to expect from day to day and certainly doesn't feel safe." Those same feelings used to plague Nick while he was growing up.

"I've dealt with kids like that."

"In a perfect world, Ned wouldn't drink and would love Corey unconditionally. But that isn't going to happen. Ned isn't going to change." He knew firsthand the mind-set of an alcoholic and remembered the times his dad promised to stop drinking and reform. He never did; in fact he got worse.

"How do you know that for sure?"

"I just do." He didn't share his past with anyone. It was a part of his life he wanted to wipe from his mind, but it was always there in the background. He never wanted to see a child grow up the way he had.

"Then I'll pray for the best for Corey," Darcy said.

"The best scenario would be the state taking Corey away from Ned and a good family adopting him. I wish I was in a position to do it." The second he said that last sentence he wanted to snatch it back. He had no business being anyone's father.

"Because you're single? That might not matter in certain cases."

"I'm not dad material." How could he explain that he was struggling to erase the debt that his father had accumulated? If he lost the ranch, he would lose his home and job. But, more important, what if he wasn't a good father to Corey? It was one thing to be there to help when needed, but it was very different to be totally responsible for raising a child.

Don't miss
THE COWBOY'S TEXAS FAMILY
by Margaret Daley, available January 2017 wherever
Love Inspired® books and ebooks are sold.